SRA

Open Court Reading

Decodable Takehome Books

Level B Set 1
Books 41–75

A Division of The McGraw-Hill Companies

Columbus, Ohio

SRA/McGraw-Hill
A Division of The ***McGraw-Hill*** *Companies*

Printed in the United States of America.

Send all inquiries to:
SRA/McGraw-Hill
8787 Orion Place
Columbus, OH 43240-4027

ISBN 0-02-683928-8

19 20 21 22 23 QPD 10 09 08 07 06

Contents

Level B Set 1, Books 41–75

About the Decodable Takehome Books

The *SRA Open Court Reading Decodable Books* allow your students to apply their knowledge of phonic elements to read simple, engaging texts. Each story supports instruction in a new phonic element and incorporates elements and words that have been learned earlier.

The students can fold and staple the pages of each *Decodable Takehome Book* to make books of their own to keep and read. We suggest that you keep extra sets of the stories in your classroom for the children to reread.

How to make a Decodable Takehome Book

1. Tear out the pages you need.

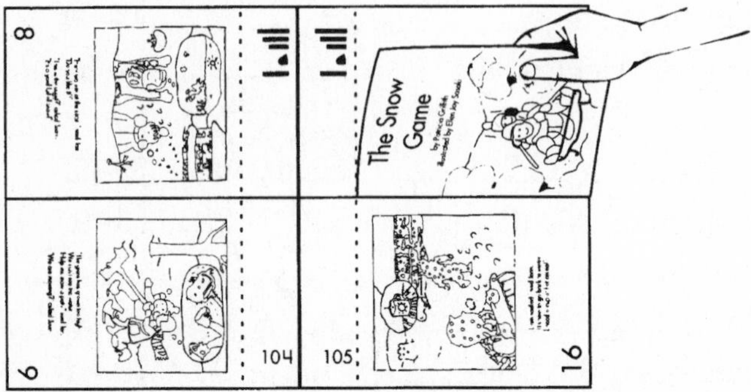

2. For 16-page stories, place pages 8 and 9, 6 and 11, 4 and 13, and 2 and 15 faceup.

or

2. For 8-page stories, place pages 4 and 5, and pages 2 and 7 faceup.

For 16-page book

3. Place the pages on top of each other in this order: pages 8 and 9, pages 6 and 11, pages 4 and 13, and pages 2 and 15.

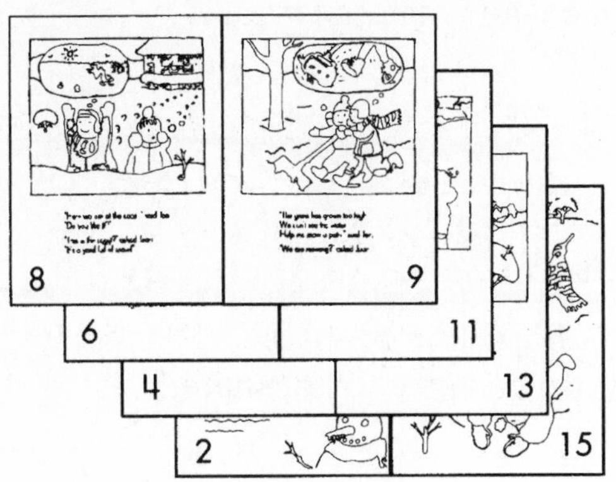

4. Fold along the center line.

5. Check to make sure the pages are in order.

6. Staple the pages along the fold.

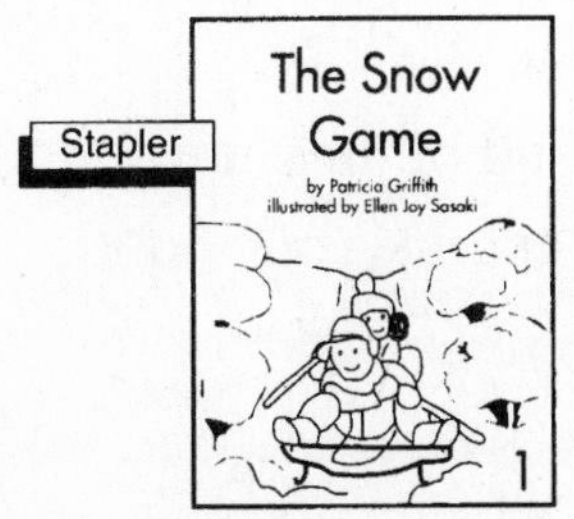

For 8-page book

3. Place pages 4 and 5 on top of pages 2 and 7.

4. Fold along the center line.

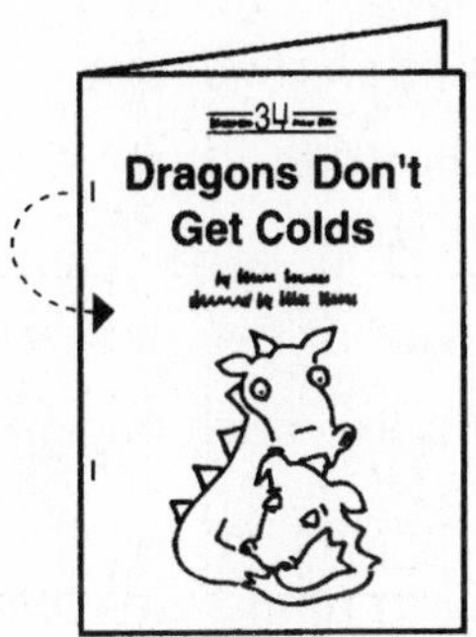

5. Check to make sure the pages are in order.

6. Staple the pages along the fold.

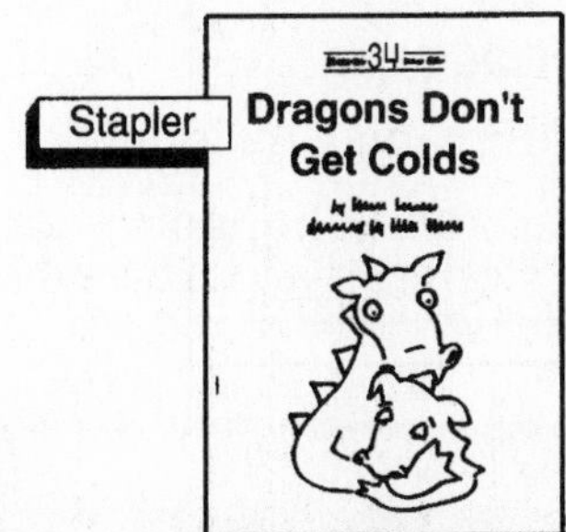

Just to let you know...

A message from ____

Help your child discover the joy of independent reading with *SRA Open Court Reading*. From time to time your child will bring home his or her very own *Decodable Takehome Books* to share with you. With your help, these stories can give your child important reading practice and a joyful shared reading experience.

You may want to set aside a few minutes every evening to read these stories together. Here are some suggestions you may find helpful:

- Do not expect your child to read each story perfectly, but concentrate on sharing the book together.
- Participate by doing some of the reading.
- Talk about the stories as you read, give lots of encouragement, and watch as your child becomes more fluent throughout the year!

Learning to read takes lots of practice. Sharing these stories is one way that your child can gain that valuable practice. Encourage your child to keep the *Decodable Takehome Books* in a special place. This collection will make a library of books that your child can read and reread. Take the time to listen to your child read from his or her library. Just a few moments of shared reading each day can give your child the confidence needed to excel in reading.

Children who read every day come to think of reading as a pleasant, natural part of life. One way to inspire your child to read is to show that reading is an important part of your life by letting him or her see you reading books, magazines, newspapers, or any other materials. Another good way to show that you value reading is to share a *Decodable Takehome Book* with your child each day.

Successful reading experiences allow children to be proud of their new-found reading ability. Support your child with interest and enthusiasm about reading. You won't regret it!

Cedric had a space in Lance's basement and a place at their table. Cedric liked the city and its citizens. Cedric ate lots of cake. Cedric became a fat and contented dragon. Cedric and Lance became friends.

SRA Open Court Reading

Lance's Dragon

by Dina McClellan
illustrated by Len Epstein

A Division of The McGraw-Hill Companies
Columbus, Ohio

SRA/McGraw-Hill

A Division of The ***McGraw-Hill*** *Companies*

Printed in the United States of America.

Send all inquiries to:
SRA/McGraw-Hill
8787 Orion Place
Columbus, OH 43240-4027

"Mom makes a great apple cake," Lance said. "We love apple cake. But Mom cannot bake cakes unless we have a flame. Can you lend us your flame? You can live with us and help make apple cakes."

Lance glanced at Cedric's ring. It was his mom's bracelet! Lance spotted the lace scarf. Lance grabbed for the bracelet and scarf. Flames licked Lance's face. Then Lance spotted something else. For a dragon, Cedric was too thin. This was Lance's big chance.

SRA
Open Court Reading

"Get up!" Lance's mom yelled.
"Cedric the Dragon was here!"
"Cedric has my silver bracelet and lace scarf!" she added.
"All citizens have had enough!"

That dragon is bad," stated Lance. Cedric must be stopped."

ance did not wish to face dragon. But Lance was mad. ance paced in a circle. Then he raced out.

Lance walked into a cave. It was as hot as a blazing sun. There were cinders all over the place. In the distance Lance could see Cedric in the center of a red-hot blaze. Lance went up to Cedric's face and felt hot flames. "That d-d-dragon is bad," Lance stammered. "I do not like this p-p-place."

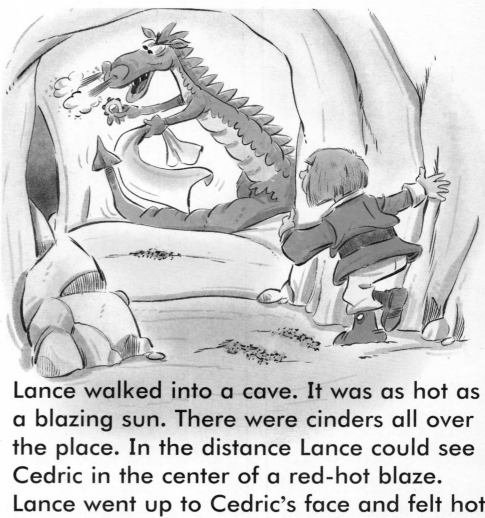

...and save a slice for me!

SRA Open Court Reading

Spice Cake

by Diane Zaga
illustrated by Deborah Colvin Borgo

A Division of The McGraw-Hill Companies
Columbus, Ohio

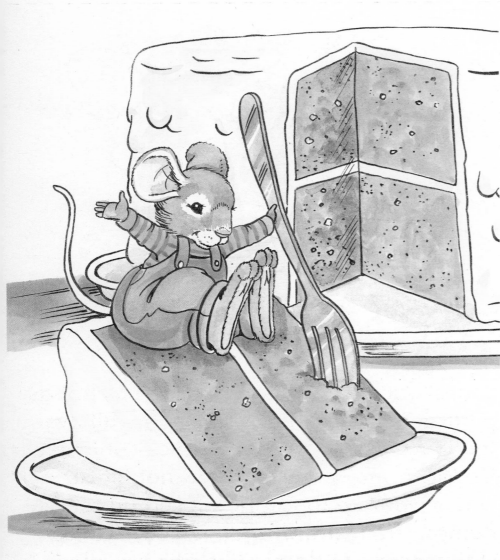

SRA/McGraw-Hill

A Division of The ***McGraw-Hill*** *Companies*

Printed in the United States of America.

Send all inquiries to:
SRA/McGraw-Hill
8787 Orion Place
Columbus, OH 43240-4027

Stir it a while.
And then bake it…

Then I'll mix in a slice or
two of a nice ripe apple.

What is this?
Spice cake?
I can make a nice spice cake, too.

I'll add a shake of this,
and a tiny pinch of that.

Next I'll add a plate of diced nuts,
and nine chopped dates.

Jake Troll went home and put on his robe.
For once, Jake Troll had no ice on his nose.
"I am not cold!" yelled Jake Troll.
"Thank you, Mole!"

SRA Open Court Reading

The Cold Troll

by Amy Goldman Koss
illustrated by Jan Pyk

A Division of The McGraw-Hill Companies
Columbus, Ohio

SRA/McGraw-Hill
A Division of The McGraw-Hill Companies

Printed in the United States of America.

Send all inquiries to:
SRA/McGraw-Hill
8787 Orion Place
Columbus, OH 43240-4027

Mole read Jake Troll's note.
"Do not mope, Troll," Mole scolded.
"Take home this robe."

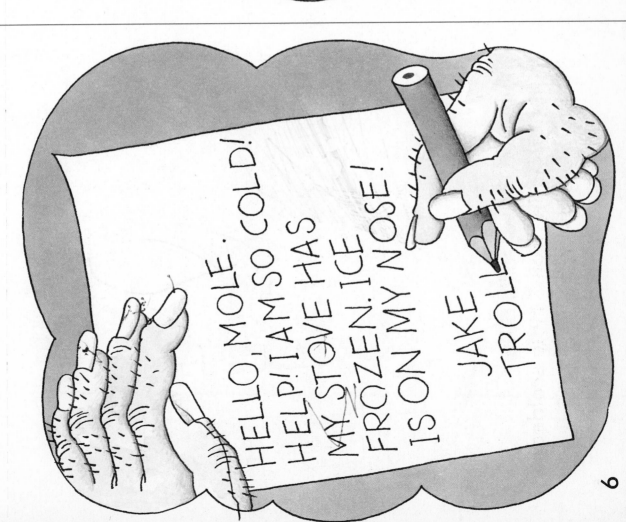

HELLO, MOLE.
HELP! I AM SO COLD!
MY STOVE HAS
FROZEN. ICE
IS ON MY NOSE!

JAKE
TROLL

Jake Troll's old home felt cold.
It was so cold that ice formed on his nose.
It was so cold that his stove froze.

Jake Troll poked his broken stove with a stick.

"This is no joke," Jake Troll said.

"This cold is too much. I have one last hope. I will go drop a note for Mole."

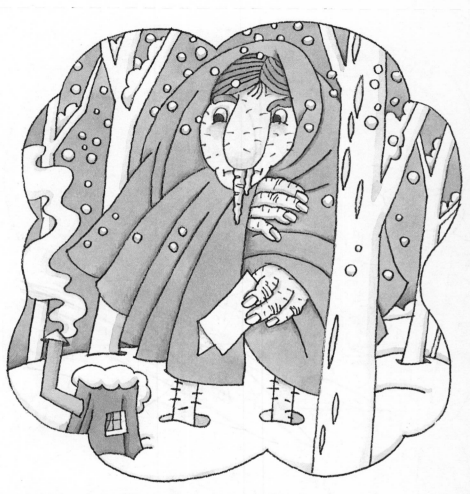

Mole had a nice snug hole.

Cold Jake Troll left a note.

He slipped the note into Mole's hole.

And Mole is
nice and warm.

SRA Open Court Reading

A Chore for Mole

by Marilyn Jager Adams
illustrated by Jan Pyk

A Division of The McGraw-Hill Companies
Columbus, Ohio

SRA/McGraw-Hill
A Division of The ***McGraw-Hill*** *Companies*

Printed in the United States of America.

Send all inquiries to:
SRA/McGraw-Hill
8787 Orion Place
Columbus, OH 43240-4027

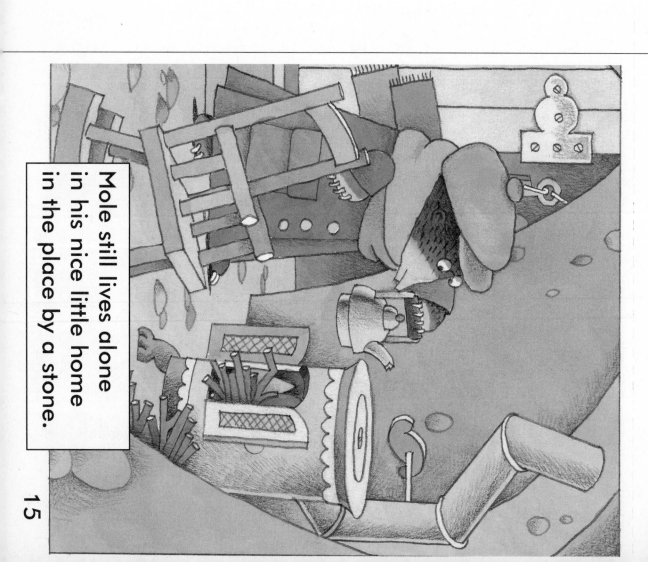

Mole still lives alone
in his nice little home
in the place by a stone.

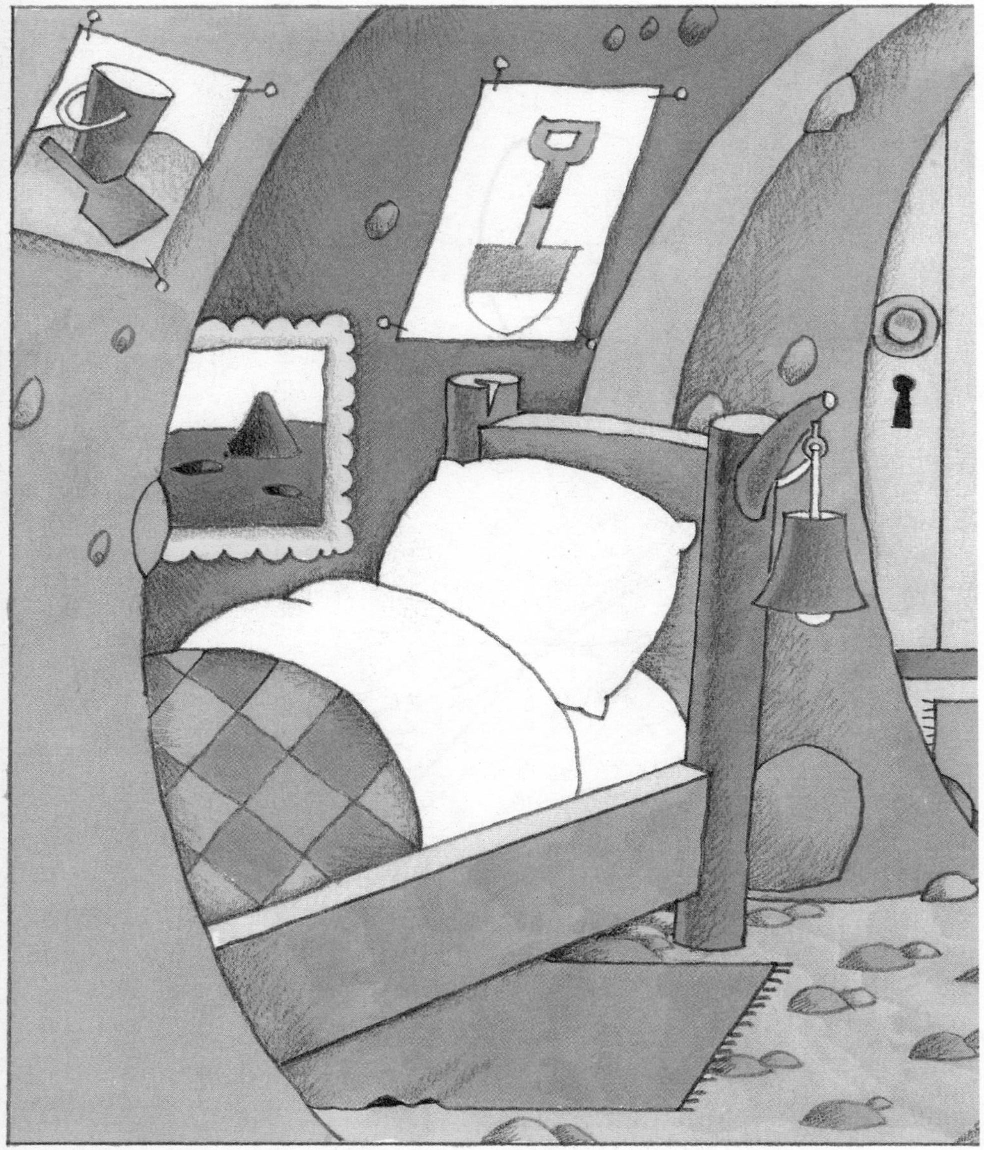

Mole's Home

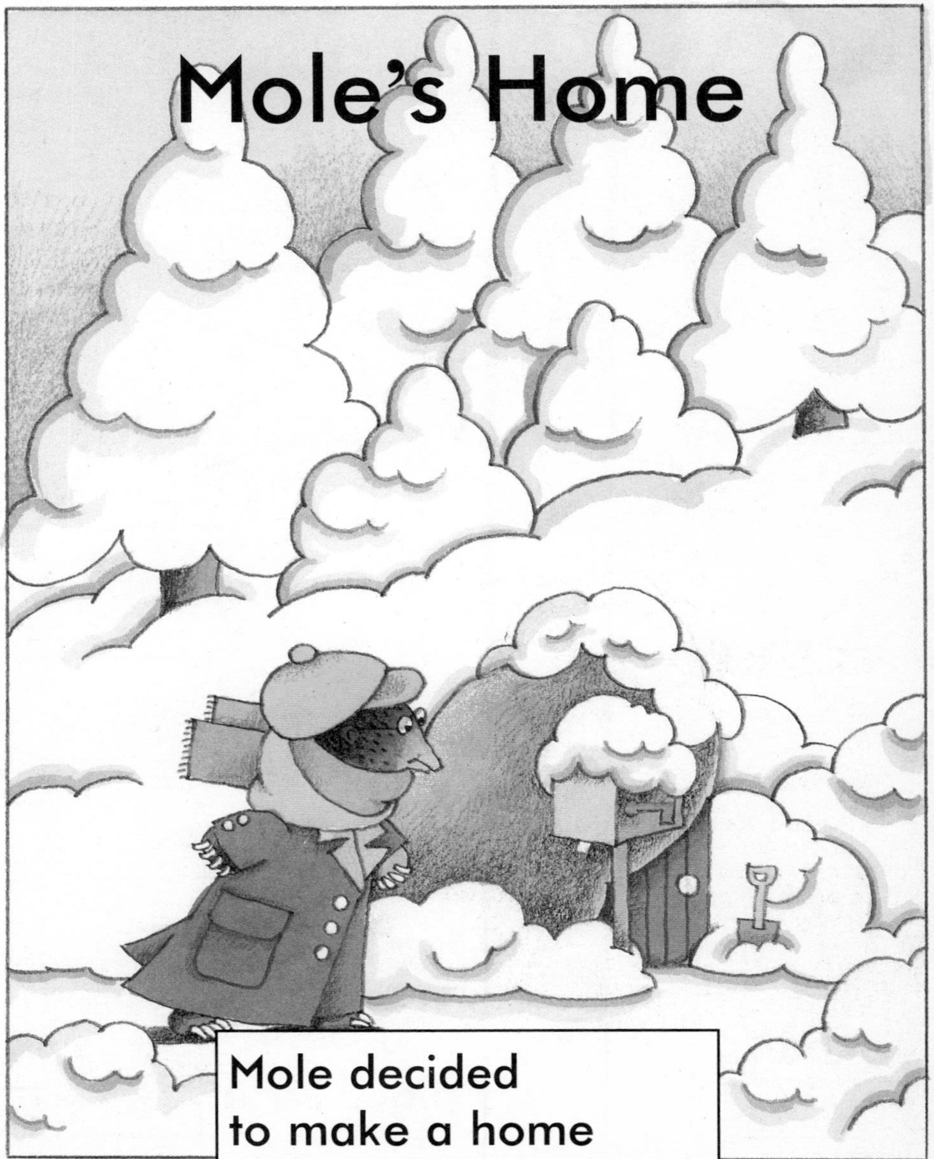

Mole decided
to make a home
in a place by a stone.

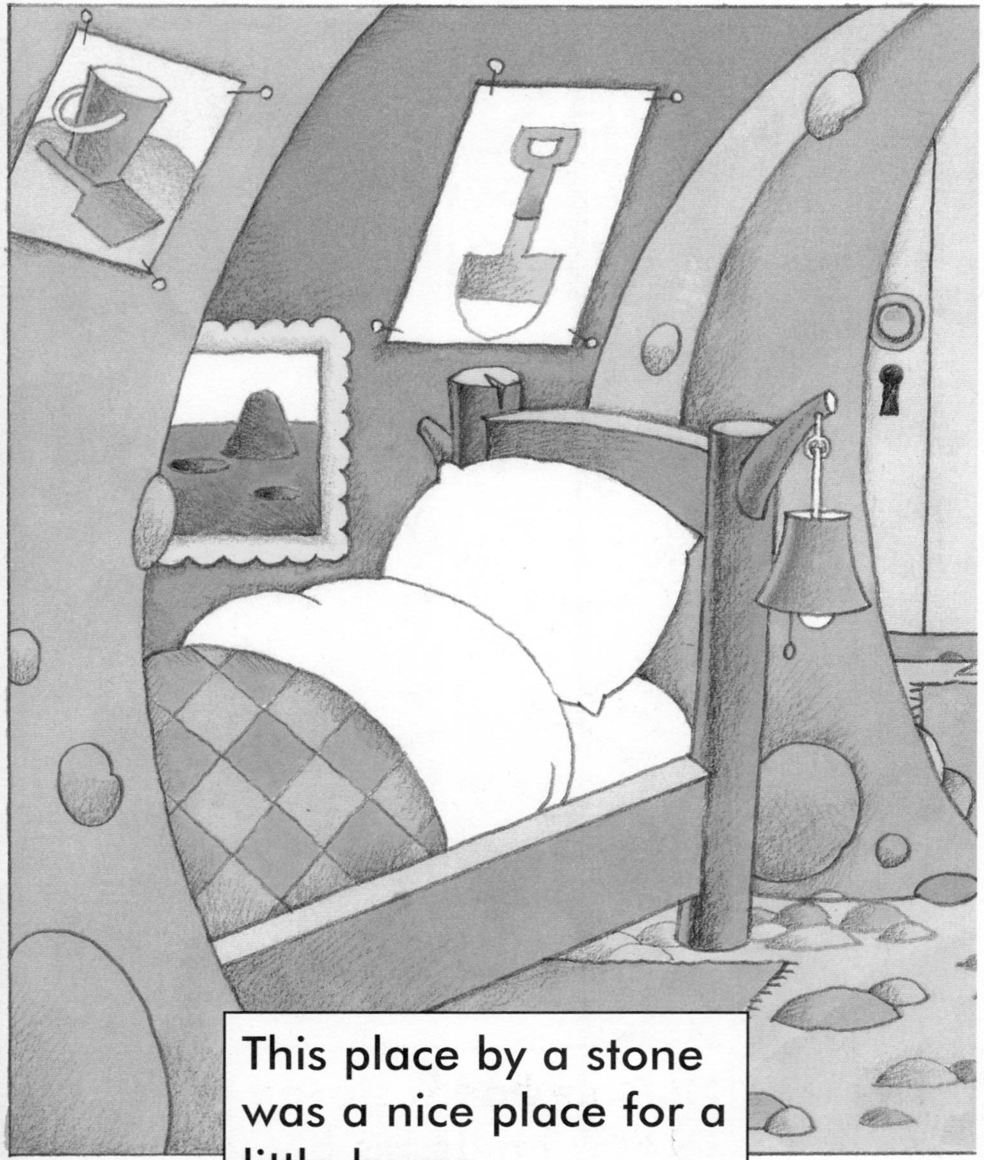

This place by a stone was a nice place for a little home.

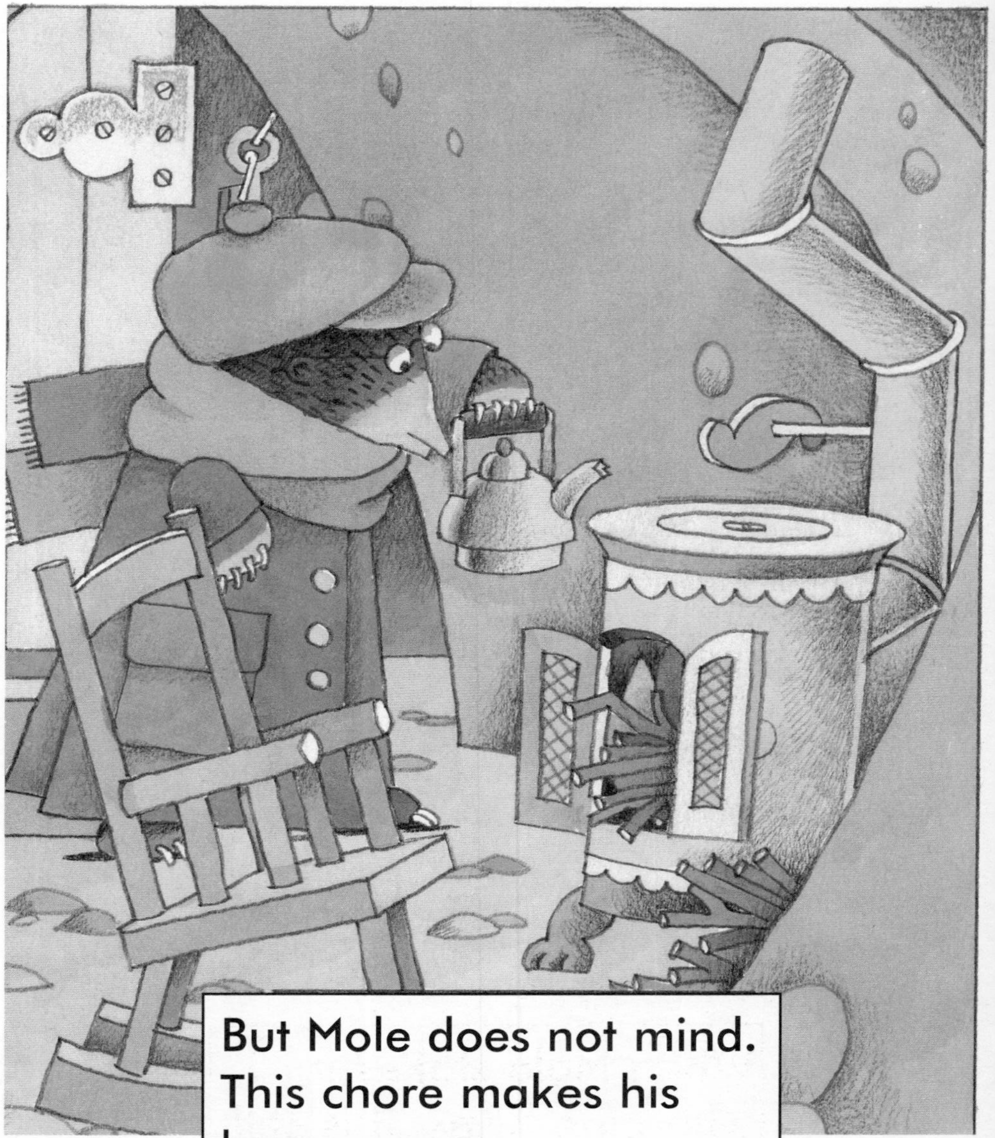

But Mole does not mind. This chore makes his home warm.

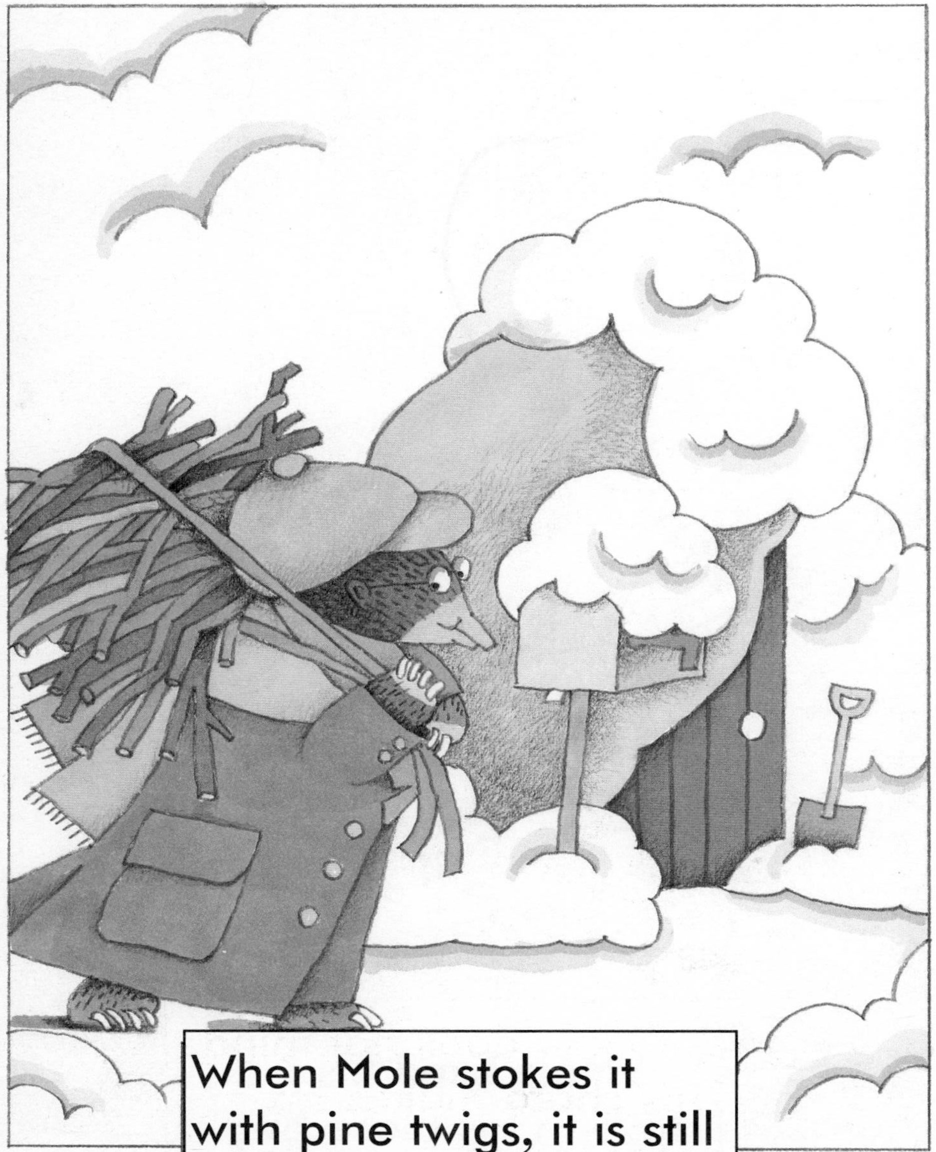

When Mole stokes it with pine twigs, it is still a big chore.

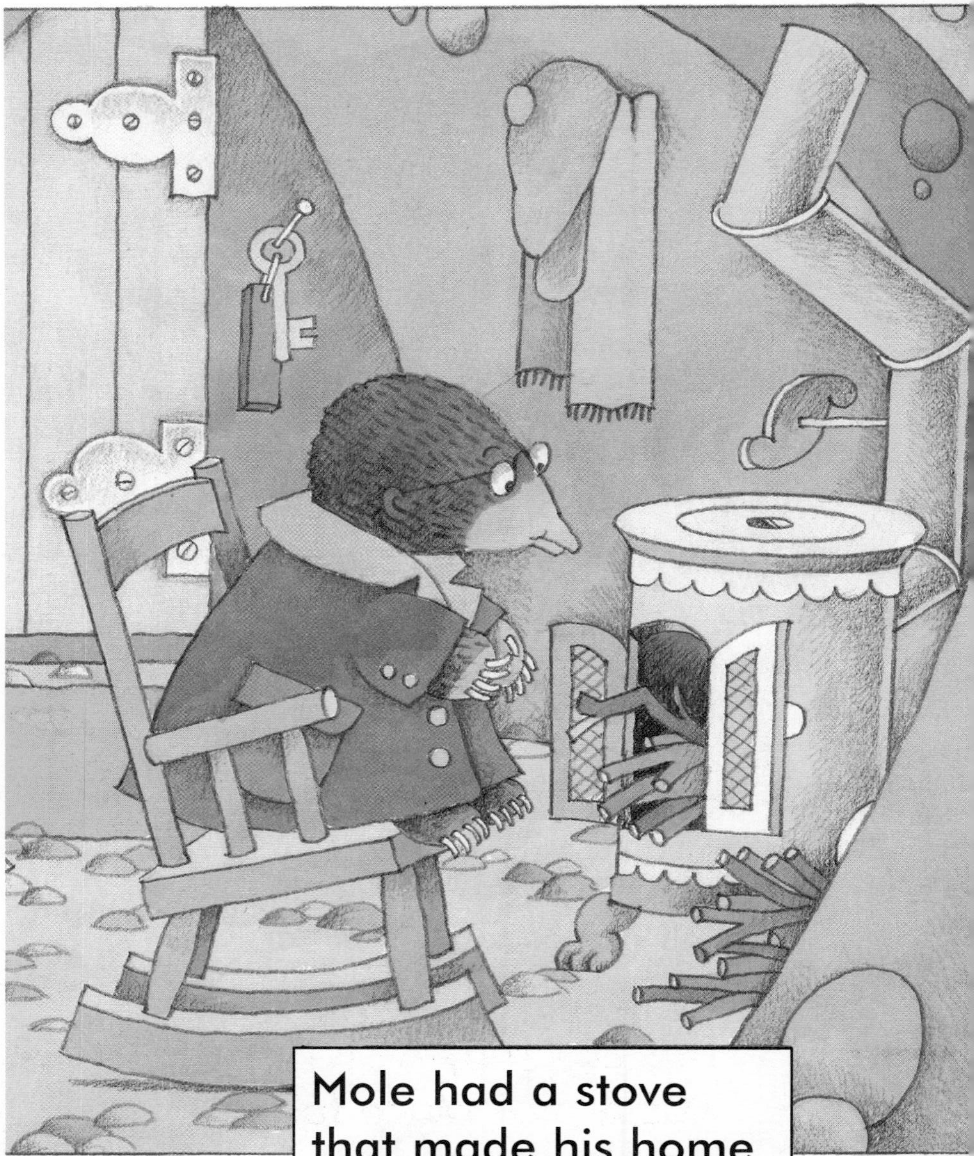

Mole had a stove that made his home warm.

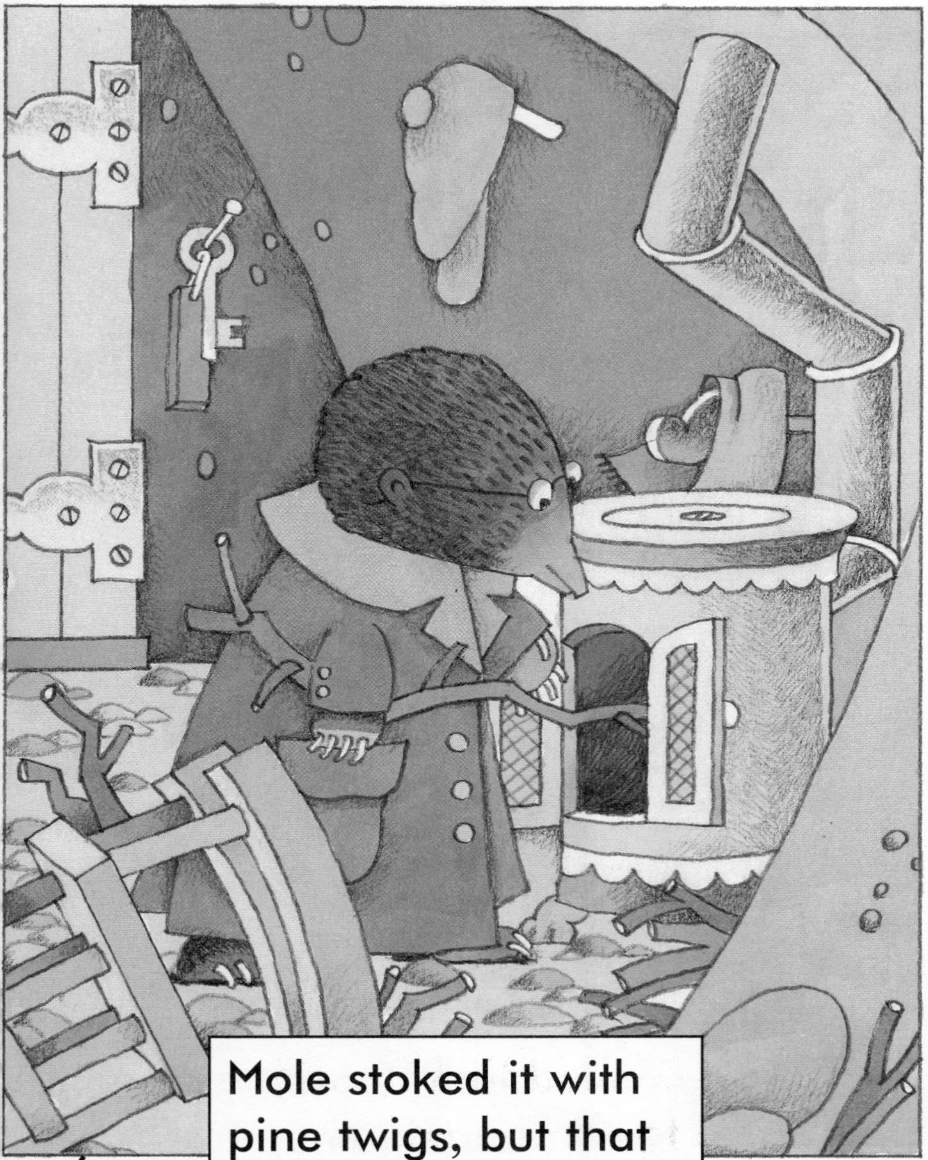

Mole stoked it with pine twigs, but that was a hard chore.

But Mole fixed his stove in his place by a stone.

Mole's Stove

Mole's face felt like ice. He was cold and chilled to his bones.

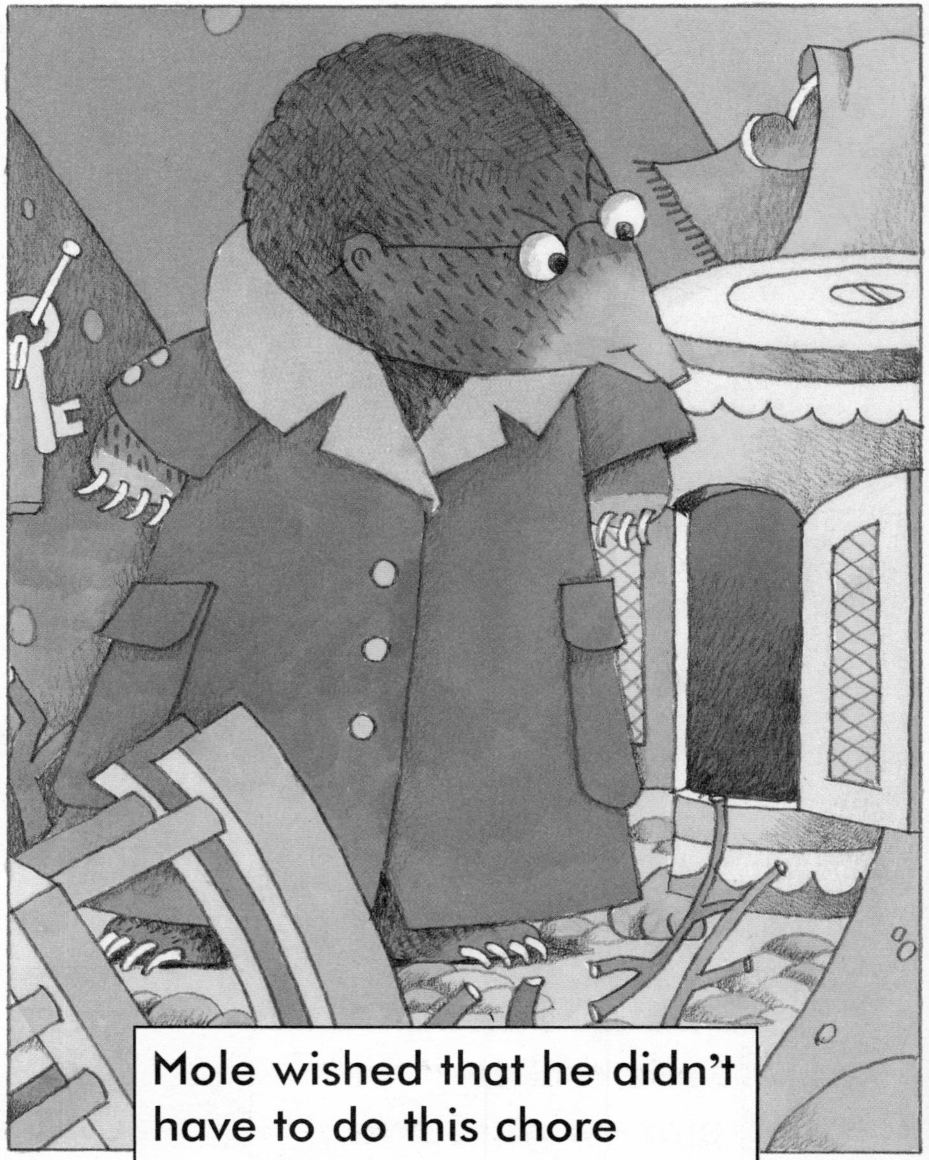

Mole wished that he didn't have to do this chore anymore.

SRA Open Court Reading

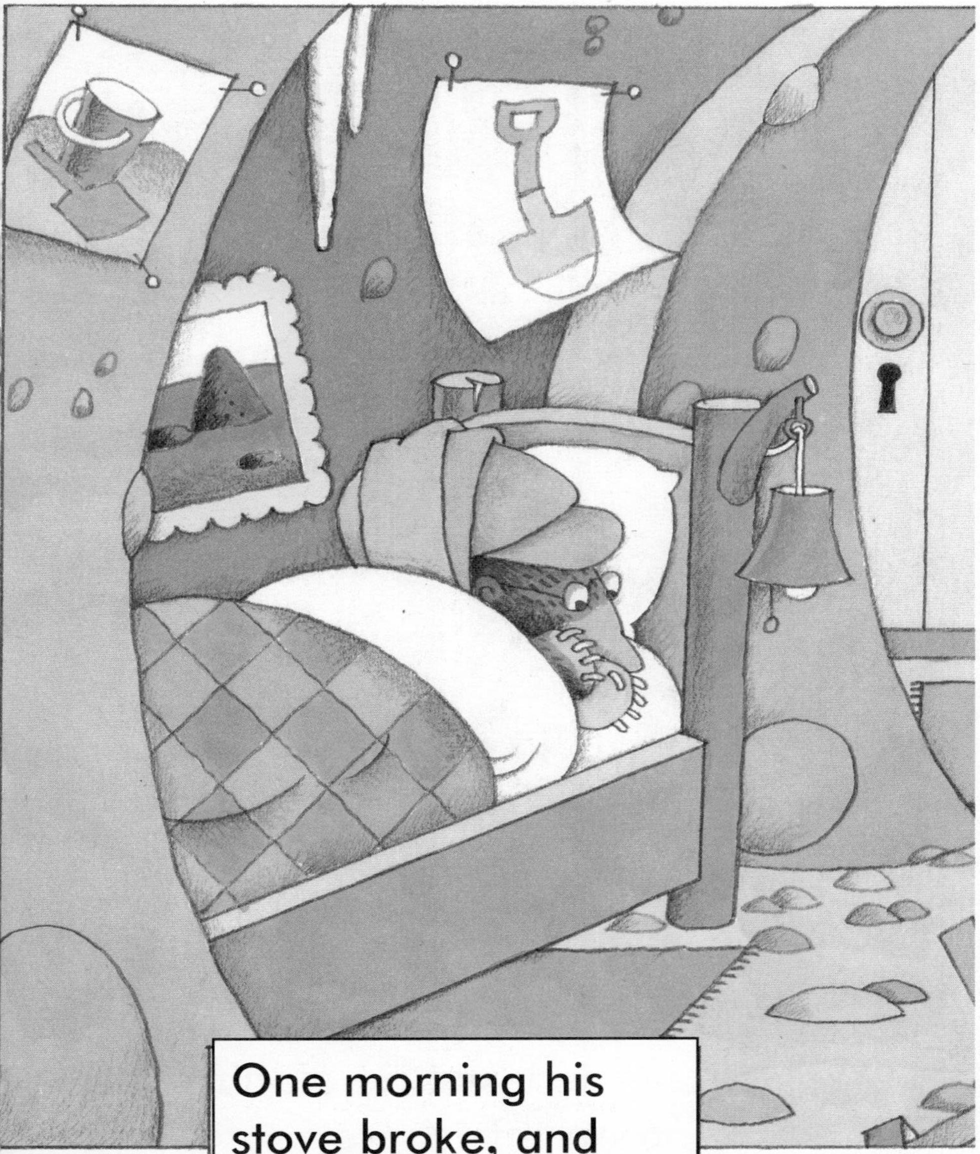

One morning his
stove broke, and
when Mole awoke,

his home in a place next to
a stone got too cold.

Val, Velvet, and Vic get in Val's van.
The vet helped Velvet and Vic get better.
Val can have fun with her cats again!

Open Court Reading

At the Vet

by Linda Taylor
illustrated by Meryl Henderson

A Division of The McGraw-Hill Companies
Columbus, Ohio

SRA/McGraw-Hill
A Division of The ***McGraw-Hill*** *Companies*

Printed in the United States of America.

Send all inquiries to:
SRA/McGraw-Hill
8787 Orion Place
Columbus, OH 43240-4027

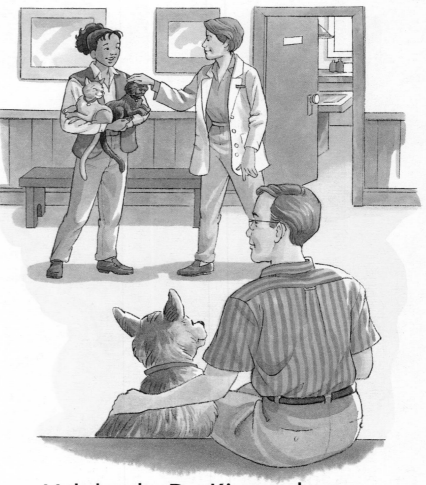

Val thanks Dr. Kim and says,
"I am glad I came.
Velvet and Vic will get well."

Dr. Kim looks at Velvet and Vic.
She states, "The cats ate a bad vine.
It made them sick."
She gives them some big white pills.

Val has two pet cats.
Velvet is a black cat.
Vic is a gold cat.

Velvet and Vic are sick today.
Val must take her cats to a vet.
Val tells her cats, "I will put on a red vest.
Then we will go in the van."

They ride in Val's van.
Velvet likes the vet.
Vic does not like the vet.
He hides in the back of Val's van.

Cupid does not like
big branches on his back.
But Cupid likes Alfonso's music!

Open Court Reading

Cupid the Mule

by Dottie Raymer
illustrated by Jan Pyk

A Division of The McGraw-Hill Companies
Columbus, Ohio

SRA/McGraw-Hill
A Division of The McGraw-Hill Companies

Printed in the United States of America.

Send all inquiries to:
SRA/McGraw-Hill
8787 Orion Place
Columbus, OH 43240-4027

At last Alfonso gets out his flute.
His flute makes nice music.

Cupid does not like branches on his back.
Cupid stands still and does not budge.

Cupid is a cute mule.
Cupid lives in a forest
close to the Maze River.

Cupid likes the forest and
the Maze River.
But Cupid likes music the most.

Alfonso is a trader.
He cuts branches
and trades them at the river.
After Alfonso cuts big branches,
he puts them on Cupid's back.

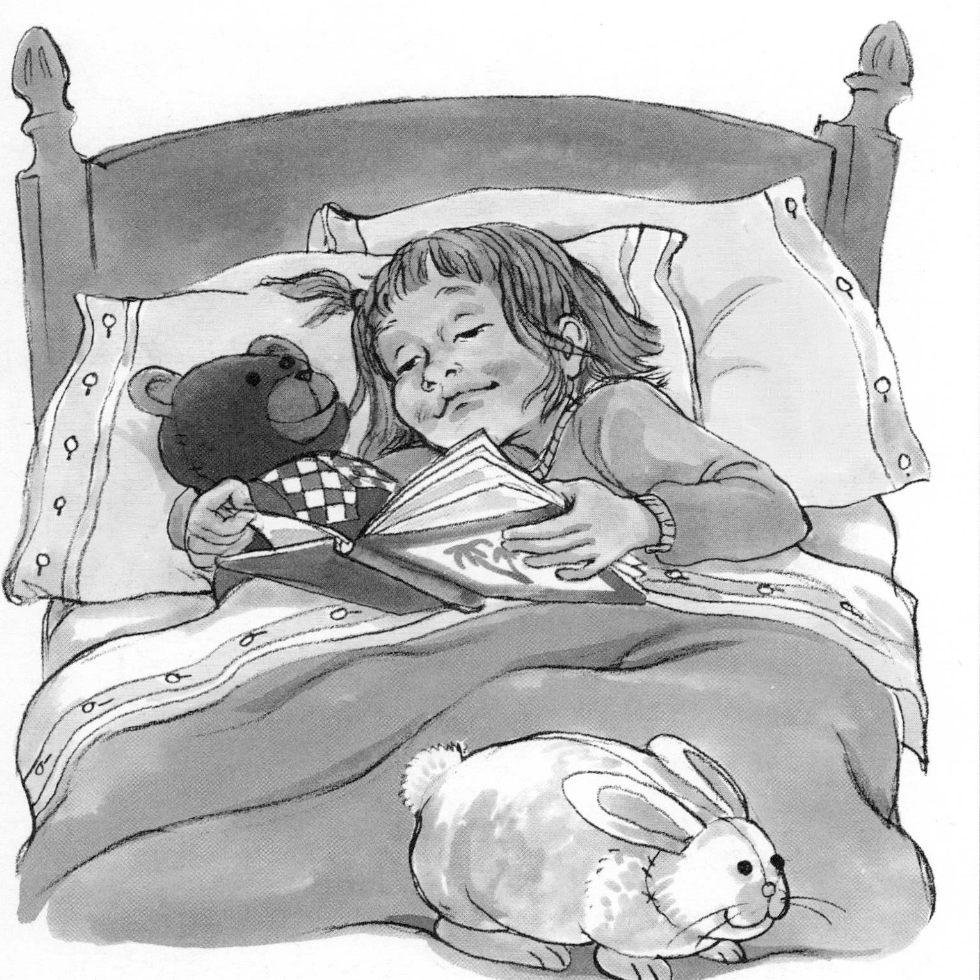

Turn a page, and a trip is finished.
I am back home in my little bed!

SRA Open Court Reading

Magic Pages

by Anne O'Brien
illustrated by Kersti Frigell

SRA
A Division of The McGraw-Hill Companies
Columbus, Ohio

SRA/McGraw-Hill

A Division of The **McGraw-Hill** *Companies*

Printed in the United States of America.

Send all inquiries to:
SRA/McGraw-Hill
8787 Orion Place
Columbus, OH 43240-4027

I can watch tan camels run
or huge giraffes standing in the sun.

I can hunt for large shells
that whisper in my ear.

When I turn magic pages,
I can take a trip.

I can travel to far lands and hunt for gems.

I can swim with sharks.
I can jump on the back of a giant whale.

"Here is the secret,"
said Steve with a smile.
"It is a kitten. It is a gift."

SRA
Open Court Reading

Steve's Secret

by Amy Goldman Koss
illustrated by Deborah Colvin Borgo

A Division of The McGraw-Hill Companies
Columbus, Ohio

SRA/McGraw-Hill

A Division of The ***McGraw-Hill*** *Companies*

Printed in the United States of America.

Send all inquiries to:
SRA/McGraw-Hill
8787 Orion Place
Columbus, OH 43240-4027

"What shade is it? Is it white?
Is it red?" asked Eve.

“What shape is it?” she asked.
“Is it flat? Is it tall?”
“It is not flat or tall,” he stated.
“But it is my secret. Let me be.”

Steve had a secret.
He hid it in a box.

"What is in that box?" asked Eve.
"Is it an acorn? Is it a stone?"
"It is a secret," said Steve.
"It is for me."

"What size is it?" asked Eve. "Is it little?
Is it big?"
"It is little," stated Steve.
"But it is a secret. Do not even ask."

June and Duke James and a mule and a giraffe and a giant smiled and became good friends.

Open Court Reading

June and the Duke

by Lisa Trumbauer
illustrated by Kersti Frigell

A Division of The McGraw-Hill Companies
Columbus, Ohio

SRA/McGraw-Hill

A Division of The McGraw-Hill Companies

Printed in the United States of America.

Send all inquiries to:
SRA/McGraw-Hill
8787 Orion Place
Columbus, OH 43240-4027

It was a huge smile!

"THEN WHAT CAN YOU DO, JUNE?" asked Duke James.
"I can be your friend," said June.
Duke James said nothing.
Then Duke James smiled.

In this small village,
there lived a Duke named James.

Duke James ruled.
But Duke James was sad.
"Who can make me smile?"
asked Duke James.

"June, can you sing a tune?"
"No, sir," spoke June.
"Can you make music on a violin or a flute?"
"No, sir," spoke June.
"Can you dance
or tell jokes?" asked Duke James.
"No, sir," stated June.

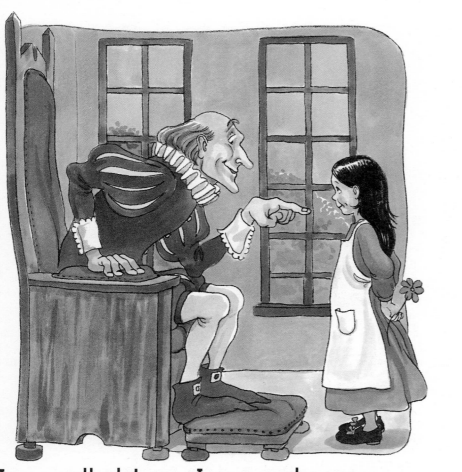

"I am called June. I can make you smile," stated June.
"That is a nice name," said Duke James, "but what can you do?"

"I can!" yelled a mule named Pete.
"I will use my lips.
I will sing a tune."

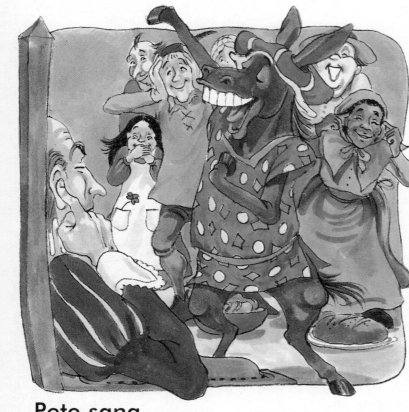

Pete sang.
Pete joked.
Pete smiled.
But Duke James was not amused.
"Who can make me smile?"
asked Duke James.

"Excuse me, Sir Duke."
Duke James expected a mule
or a giraffe or a giant.
But it was a little girl.

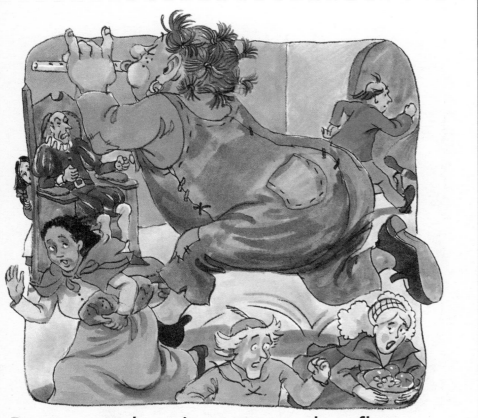

Bev created a nice tune on her flute.
Bev told many jokes.
Bev smiled,
but Duke James did not smile.
"CAN SOMEONE HERE
MAKE ME SMILE?" asked Duke James.

"I can!" called Eve Giraffe.
"I will use this violin.
I will make music for you."

Eve Giraffe made music on her violin.
Eve Giraffe danced.
Eve Giraffe smiled.
But Duke James still did not smile.
"Who can make me smile?"
asked Duke James.

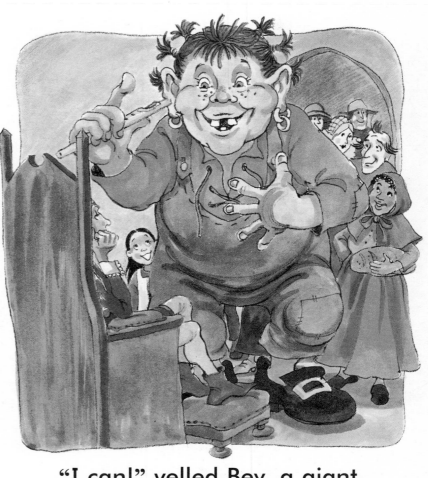

"I can!" yelled Bev, a giant.
"I will use a flute.
I will create a pretty tune.
I will tell jokes."

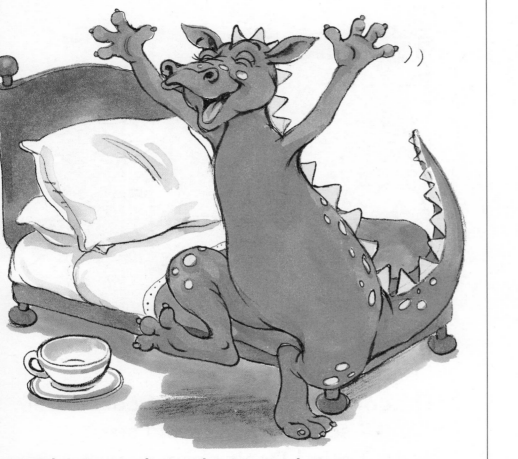

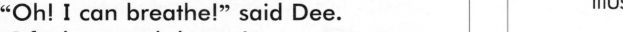

"Oh! I can breathe!" said Dee.
"I feel so much better!"
"I am glad," Dad said with a smile,
"since dragons <u>don't</u> get colds."

SRA Open Court Reading

Dragons Don't Get Colds

by Dottie Raymer
illustrated by Kersti Frigell

A Division of The McGraw-Hill Companies
Columbus, Ohio

SRA/McGraw-Hill
A Division of The **McGraw-Hill** *Companies*

Printed in the United States of America.

Send all inquiries to:
SRA/McGraw-Hill
8787 Orion Place
Columbus, OH 43240-4027

"Dragons don't like tea," creaked Dee.
"Sip it," said Dad. "We will see."
Steam tickled Dee's nose.
"Dragons don't...AH!...get...
AH!...colds!...ACHOOOO!"
Dee sneezed a <u>big</u> sneeze.

"Can <u>you</u> breathe flames?" asked Dad.
"No," creaked Dee.
Dad made a pot of tea.
"This tea's heat will help you breathe," he said.

Dee the dragon felt terrible.
"I feel weak," grumbled Dee.
"My nose hurts, and I can't breathe.
I can't speak. I just creak!"

Dee's dad felt her cheeks.
"You feel hot," he said.
"You must have a fever and a cold."

"Dragons don't get colds," creaked Dee.
"Dragons breathe hot flames."

The fancy party is over.
Nellie's babies and teddies are muddy.
The candy is dirty, and party hats are torn.
Happy puppies lap up melted ice cream.
"Thanks for the help," Willy tells his puppies.

SRA Open Court Reading

The Fancy Party

by Anne O'Brien
illustrated by Olivia Cole

SRA
A Division of The McGraw-Hill Companies
Columbus, Ohio

SRA/McGraw-Hill
A Division of The ***McGraw-Hill*** *Companies*

Printed in the United States of America.

Send all inquiries to:
SRA/McGraw-Hill
8787 Orion Place
Columbus, OH 43240-4027

Nellie gets out candy and ice cream. Willy begins to put ice cream on each plate. "No more help, please!" Nellie tells Willy's puppies.

Nellie has red berries from her garden. Willy puts a big berry on every plate. Willy's puppies help.

SRA Open Court Reading

Nellie and Willy like to have fancy parties. They invite Nellie's baby dolls and teddies. Today Willy's puppies are invited, too.

Nellie sets up a table in her yard.
Willy puts napkins and plates
on the table.
Willy's puppies help.

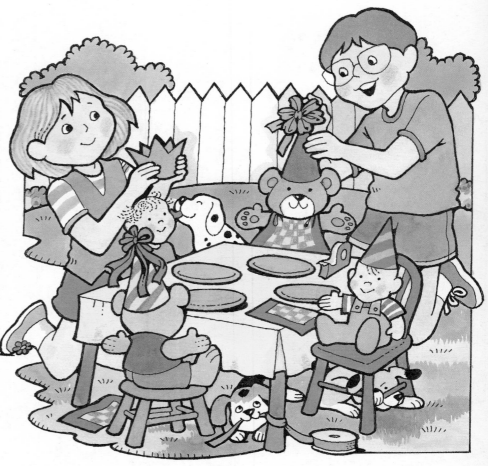

Nellie makes funny party hats.
Willy tapes ribbons onto each hat.
Willy's puppies help.

"Yes," said Miss Fay. "But for sailing,
you should stay <u>out</u> of the water!
Here comes the rain, Ray.
Grab a pail! It's time for us to bail!"

SRA
Open Court Reading

Sail Day

by Alice Cary
illustrated by Kersti Frigell

SRA
A Division of The McGraw-Hill Companies
Columbus, Ohio

SRA/McGraw-Hill
A Division of The **McGraw-Hill** *Companies*

Printed in the United States of America.

Send all inquiries to:
SRA/McGraw-Hill
8787 Orion Place
Columbus, OH 43240-4027

"A main? A jib?
I just want to sail, Miss Fay."

"A main?" asked Ray.

"Each sail has a name,"
Miss Fay told Ray. "This little one
is called a jib."

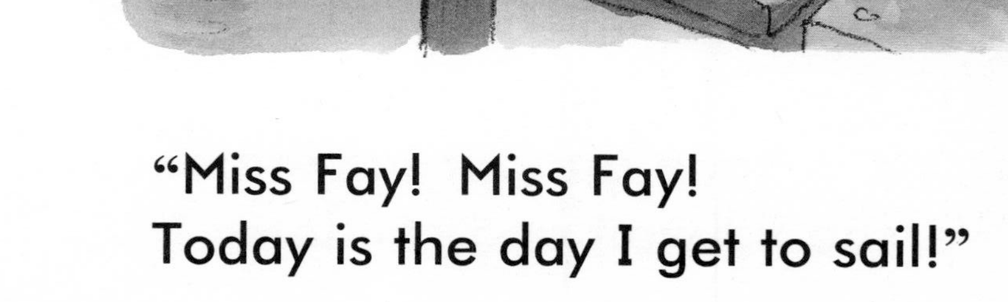

"Miss Fay! Miss Fay!
Today is the day I get to sail!"

"Hi, Ray. Yes, this is the day.
But it is quite gray. It may rain.
We should wait and sail later."

"Oh, I'm not afraid of rain.
We can sail in a little rain!"

"We can sail, but we must be safe,"
explained Miss Fay. "Stay here, Ray.
I'll check the main."

“It is time for sleep,” she tells her babies.
“We might play again tonight.”

Open Court Reading

Open Court Reading

The Opossum at Night

by Anne O’Brien
illustrated by Deborah Colvin Borgo

A Division of The McGraw-Hill Companies
Columbus, Ohio

SRA/McGraw-Hill
A Division of The **McGraw-Hill** *Companies*

Printed in the United States of America.

Send all inquiries to:
SRA/McGraw-Hill
8787 Orion Place
Columbus, OH 43240-4027

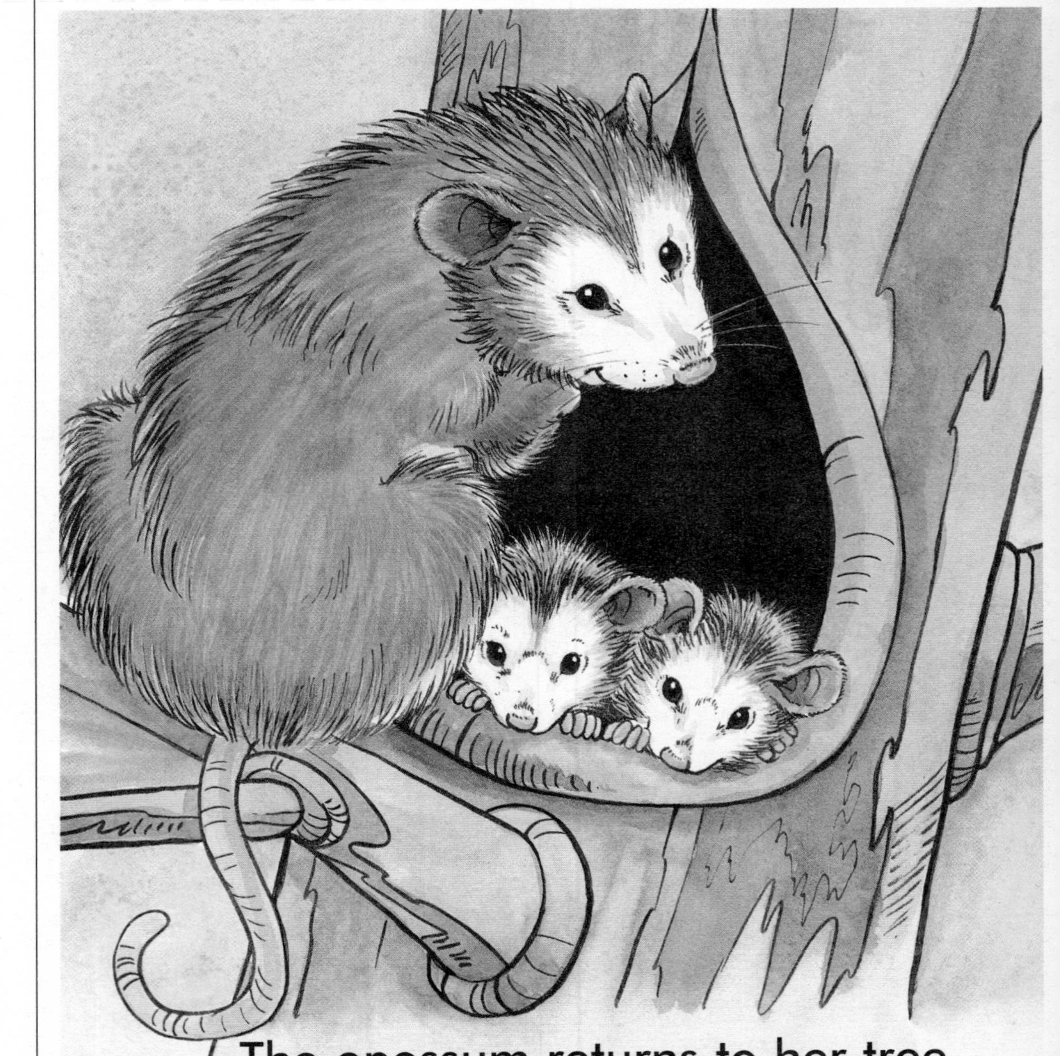

The opossum returns to her tree.
Her babies are waiting.

SRA Open Court Reading

Night is over. It begins to get light.

Mrs. Opossum does not like the light.
It is too bright. She sees better at night.

When it is night, she wakes.
She hunts for insects to feed her babies.

A dog frightens the opossum.
The opossum freezes. She stays still
and plays dead.
She "plays opossum."

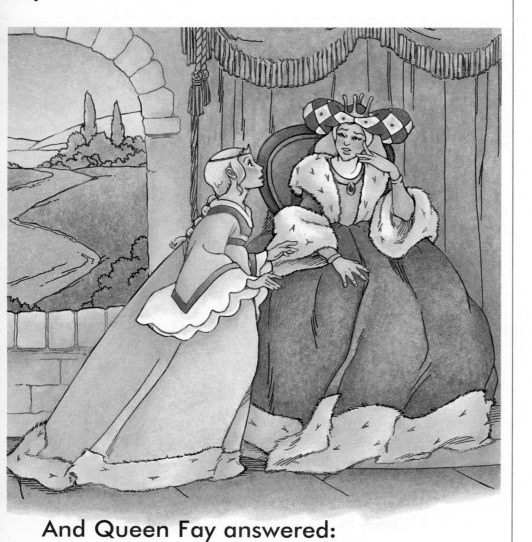

And Queen Fay answered:
"You need not tell me that!
King Ray is never on time to dine!"

SRA Open Court Reading

The King Who Was Late

by Karen Herzoff
illustrated by Anthony Accardo

A Division of The McGraw-Hill Companies
Columbus, Ohio

SRA/McGraw-Hill
A Division of The McGraw-Hill Companies

Printed in the United States of America.

Send all inquiries to:
SRA/McGraw-Hill
8787 Orion Place
Columbus, OH 43240-4027

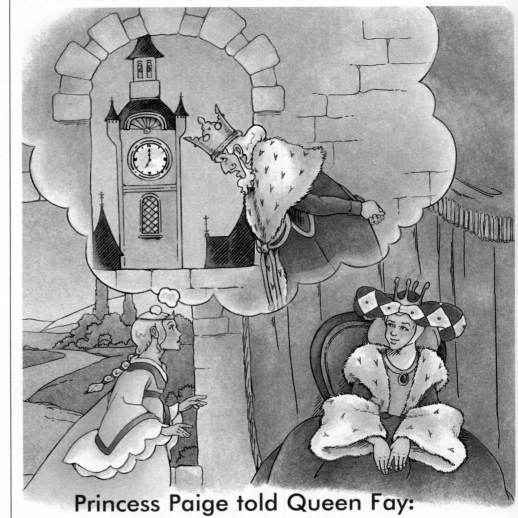

Princess Paige told Queen Fay:
"King Ray may not be on time
to dine tonight."

SRA Open Court Reading

Prince Henry told Princess Paige: "Tell Queen Fay that King Ray may add the right spice and make a fine dinner this night."

The Message

King Ray was late.
"My wife will be mad
if I make her wait," he said.
"I must tell her that I will be late."

So King Ray told his Page:
"Please tell Queen Fay that I may not be on time for dinner tonight."

The Maid told Prince Henry:
"Tell Queen Fay that
King Ray might fight thieves twice before dinner this night."

His Page told a Squire:
"Tell Queen Fay that King Ray may put on a bright leaf for dinner tonight."

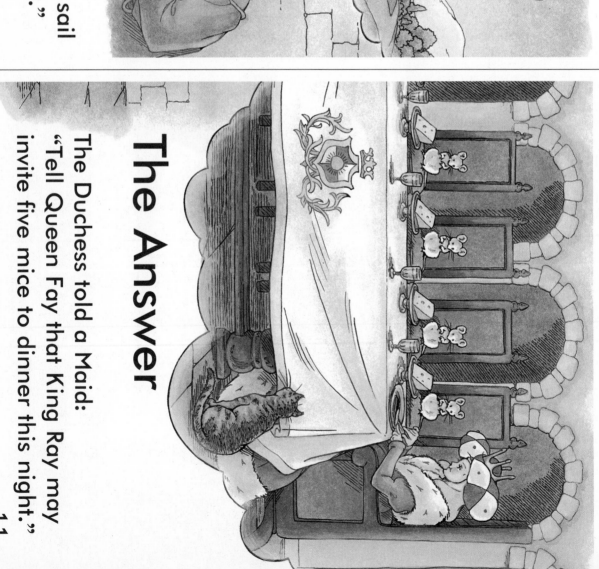

The Squire told Lord Jay:
"Tell Queen Fay that King Ray may sail a fancy kite before dinner this night."

The Answer

The Duchess told a Maid:
"Tell Queen Fay that King Ray may invite five mice to dinner this night."

Lord Jay told a Mayor:
"Tell Queen Fay that King Ray may have berries on ice for dinner this night."

The Mayor told a Duchess:
"Tell Queen Fay that King Ray may need some nice rice for dinner this night."

"It is hot and dry out here," Bly says.
"I feel better with my head stuck in the sand.
I will stay just the way I am."

SRA Open Court Reading

Why, Bly?

by Dottie Raymer
illustrated by Kersti Frigell

A Division of The McGraw-Hill Companies
Columbus, Ohio

SRA/McGraw-Hill
*A Division of The **McGraw-Hill** Companies*

Printed in the United States of America.

Send all inquiries to:
SRA/McGraw-Hill
8787 Orion Place
Columbus, OH 43240-4027

"Bly, why do you stick your head in dry sand?" cries a child. "Are you shy?"

"I am not shy," Bly replies.

SRA Open Court Reading

"Bly, why do you stick your head in dry sand?" cries Eagle. "Why not fly in the sky like me?"

"I can't fly. I am too big," replies Bly. "I like myself just the way I am."

Bly is an ostrich. She has a small head. She likes to stick her head in dry sand. Most animals feel that Bly is an odd bird.

“Bly, why do you stick your head
n dry sand?” cries Snake.
“Why not lie in the hot sun like me?”

“I do not like to lie in the hot sun,” Bly replies.
“I like myself just the way I am.”

“Bly, why do you stick your head
in dry sand?” cries Chimp.
“Why not climb a tree like me?”

“I do not want to climb trees,” Bly replies.
“I like myself the way I am.”

This doe is not a foe!
Farmer Joe drops his hoe.
He cannot be mad at this doe.
He and the doe can both have
tomatoes now.

Open Court Reading

The Farmer and the Doe

by Lisa Trumbauer
illustrated by Meryl Henderson

A Division of The McGraw-Hill Companies
Columbus, Ohio

SRA/McGraw-Hill
A Division of The McGraw-Hill Companies

Printed in the United States of America.

Send all inquiries to:
SRA/McGraw-Hill
8787 Orion Place
Columbus, OH 43240-4027

Farmer Joe stops.
He does not see a doe,
but he sees his tomatoes.
Where is that doe?

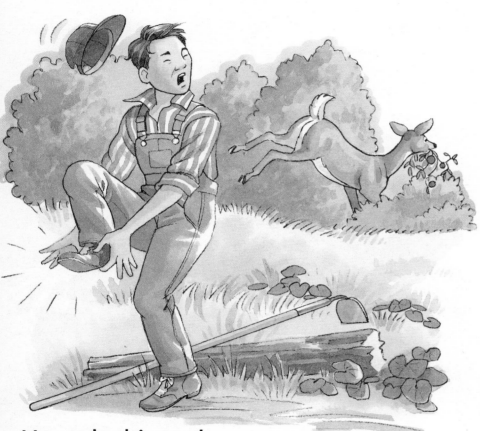

He stubs his toe!
That doe brings woe to Farmer Joe.
There goes that doe!
Farmer Joe did not want that doe
to eat his tomatoes!

SRA
Open Court
Reading

Farmer Joe checks his crops.
They are ripe!
It is time to pick tomatoes!
Farmer Joe gets his hoe.

A doe gets his tomatoes first.
The doe likes Farmer Joe's tomatoes.
But Farmer Joe does not like this doe.
This doe is his foe, not his friend.

The doe spots Farmer Joe. Oh, no!
She runs away with some tomatoes!
Farmer Joe runs after her.
He waves his hoe.

“Crow and Goat, that boat has no sail!
Grab both oars!”
yelled Boar from the shore.
“Oh, no,” groaned Goat,
“I think we MUST row!”

A Crow, a Goat, and a Boat

by Marilee Robin Burton
illustrated by Len Epstein

A Division of The McGraw-Hill Companies
Columbus, Ohio

SRA/McGraw-Hill

A Division of The McGraw-Hill Companies

Printed in the United States of America.

Send all inquiries to:
SRA/McGraw-Hill
8787 Orion Place
Columbus, OH 43240-4027

"This is not a great boat,"
mumbled Crow with a moan.
"All it does is just float,"
grumbled Goat with a groan.

But the wind did not blow, and
the boat did not go.
It did not go fast, and it did not go slow.

A crow and a goat sailed in a boat.
Their goal was the shore.
A crow and a goat hoped to see a
toad and a boar.

"I want to go fast, not slow!" said Goat.
"We shall soar in this boat!"
boasted Crow.

"Oh, let strong winds blow!"
bellowed Goat to Crow.
"Here we go! Here we go!"

Tommy True blew and blew—until he turned blue. And not a peep was heard.

Open Court Reading

Tommy True's Tuba

by Tim Paulson
illustrated by Kersti Frigell

A Division of The McGraw-Hill Companies
Columbus, Ohio

SRA/McGraw-Hill

A Division of The McGraw-Hill Companies

Printed in the United States of America.

Send all inquiries to:
SRA/McGraw-Hill
8787 Orion Place
Columbus, OH 43240-4027

Tommy took all the clothes from the line,
and he stuffed them in his tuba.
"It will not make a racket now," he claimed.

Tommy True blew and blew—until he turned blue. And not a peep was heard.

Open Court Reading

Tommy True's Tuba

by Tim Paulson
illustrated by Kersti Frigell

A Division of The McGraw-Hill Companies
Columbus, Ohio

SRA/McGraw-Hill
A Division of The McGraw-Hill Companies

Printed in the United States of America.

Send all inquiries to:
SRA/McGraw-Hill
8787 Orion Place
Columbus, OH 43240-4027

Tommy took all the clothes from the line,
and he stuffed them in his tuba.
"It will not make a racket now," he claimed.

"I am soaked," grumbled Joan.
"It's time to go back to winter.
I need a cup of hot cocoa!"

Open Court Reading

The Snow Game

by Patricia Griffith
illustrated by Ellen Joy Sasaki

A Division of The McGraw-Hill Companies
Columbus, Ohio

SRA/McGraw-Hill

A Division of The ***McGraw-Hill*** *Companies*

Printed in the United States of America.

Send all inquiries to:
SRA/McGraw-Hill
8787 Orion Place
Columbus, OH 43240-4027

"Whoa!"

Open Court Reading

More Snow

"Oh, no," moaned Joe. "New snow!"
"More snow?" cried Joan.
"No! Not more snow!"

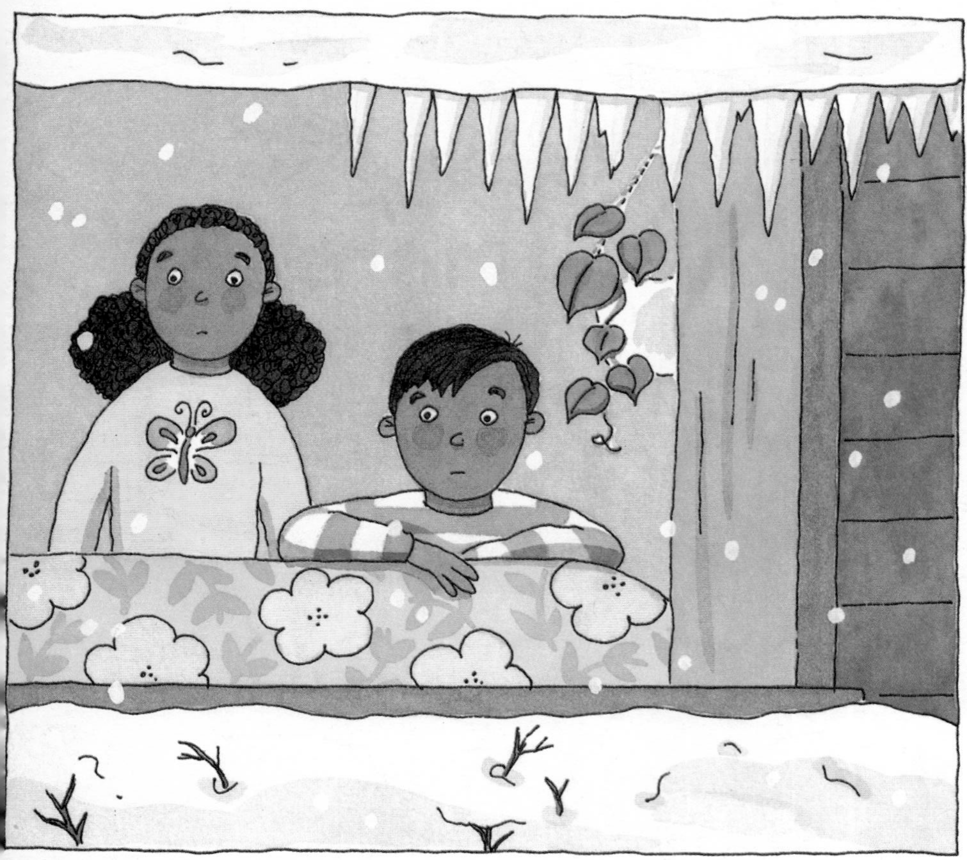

"Snow is on the sidewalks.
Snow is on the roads.
Snow is everywhere!" said Joe.

"Okay, then we'll just float.
We'll let the wind blow us.
I'll just push us off," said Joe.

"<u>Blow</u> us? Without a sail?" asked Joan.

"Okay, then follow me.
We will go on a boat!
Here are some oars," said Joe.

"Joe, you can't row in snow!" snickered Joan.

"I'm tired of winter and being cold.
And I'm tired of deep snow!"
moaned Joan.

"Why? We could make a snowman or go sledding," said Joe.

"I'm tired of snowmen and sledding," muttered Joan. "I just want it to be summer."

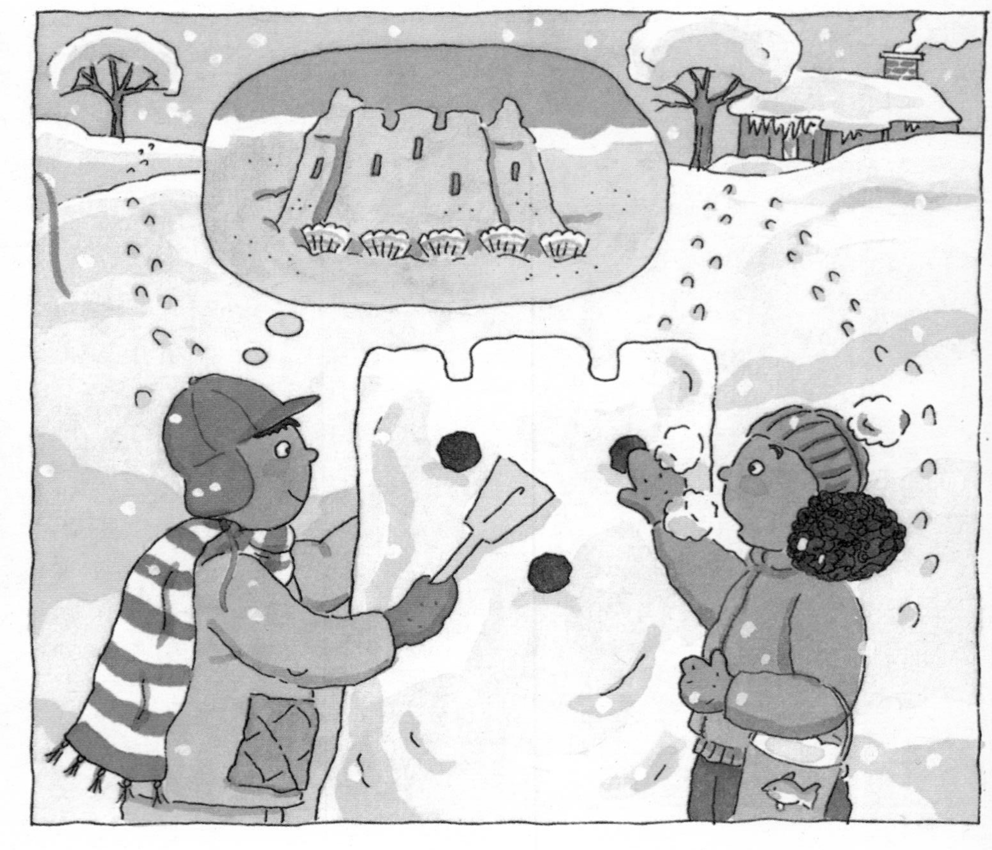

"Here, I'll show you," said Joe. "Take this pail and three pieces of coal."

"It still looks like a snowman," said Joan.

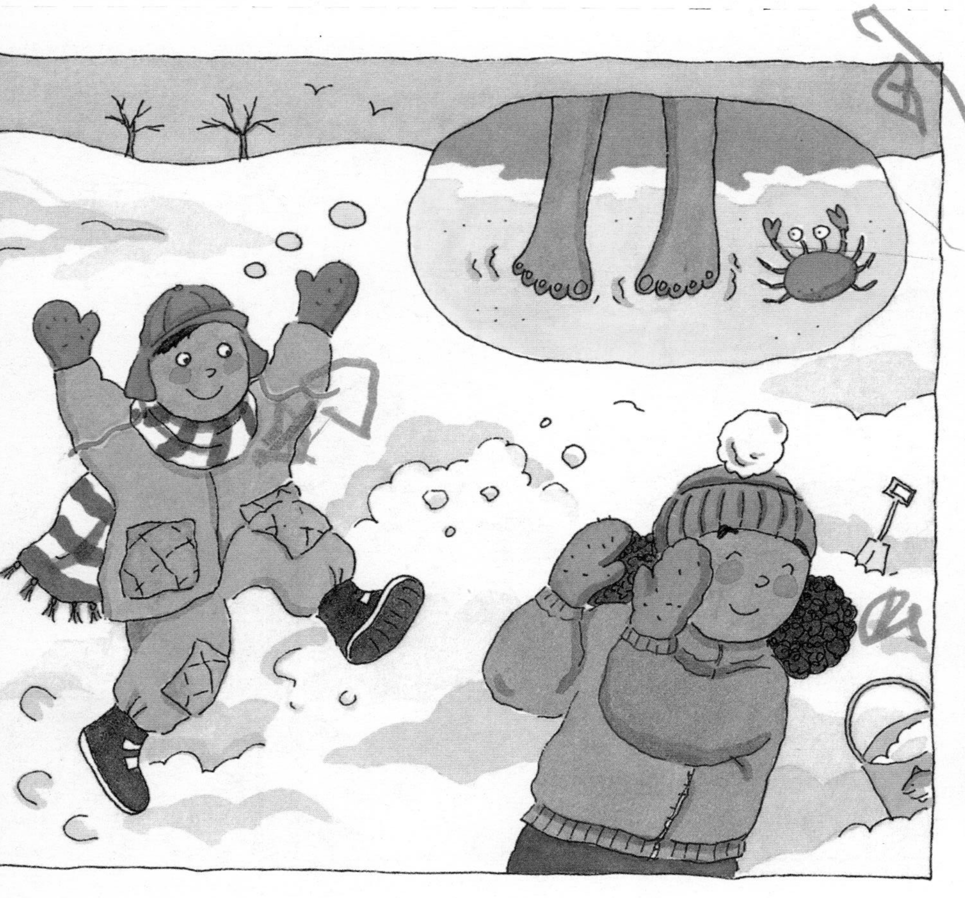

"This sand is so hot.
Wiggle your toes in it.
We'll make a sand castle," said Joe.

"A sand castle?" asked Joan.

"Okay," Joe told Joan. "Then
we will make summer come.
We will go to the beach.
Get your coat. Here we go."

At the Beach

"Here we are at the coast.
See the hot sun in the sky?
Do you like it?" asked Joe.

"This is not the <u>coast</u>," argued Joan.
"It's a yard full of white snow!"

"The grass has grown too high.
We can't see the blue water.
Help me mow a path," said Joe.

"We are <u>mowing</u>?" asked Joan.

"No, I think I'm getting a tube of toothpaste or a tuba," I moaned.

"You need better clues!" June said. "Toothpaste is a terrible birthday gift!"

SRA Open Court Reading

Birthday Clues

by Laura Kirsch
illustrated by Deborah Colvin Borgo

SRA
A Division of The McGraw-Hill Companies
Columbus, Ohio

SRA/McGraw-Hill
A Division of The **McGraw-Hill** *Companies*

Printed in the United States of America.

Send all inquiries to:
SRA/McGraw-Hill
8787 Orion Place
Columbus, OH 43240-4027

"Did your mom and dad get your newest clue?
Will you get a new bike?" asked June.

"Maybe he wants a tube of toothpaste," said Dad. "Toothpaste can be blue, but it is not big."

"No, silly," chuckled Mom. "Andrew wants a tuba for his birthday. A tuba is really big."

"But I've never seen a blue tuba," said Dad.

"This is what I wish for my birthday," I said.

"Tell your mom and dad," said June. "Your birthday is soon."

"I did. I left them a note with a clue," I said.

"Big and blue?
What is big and blue?"
asked Andrew's dad.

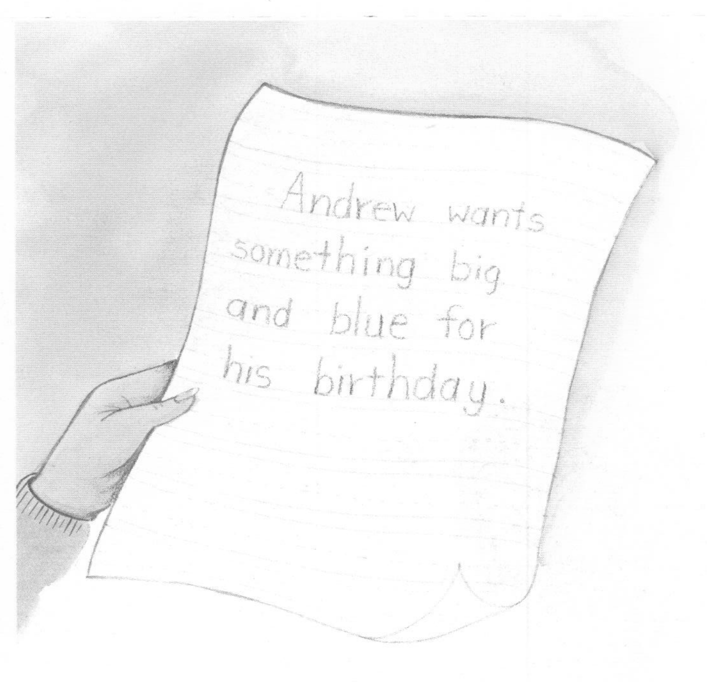

Andrew wants
something big
and blue for
his birthday.

"A balloon! That must be it!
He wants a big, blue balloon," said Mom.

"I must try a new clue," whispered
Andrew to himself.

Bunny took his joke book and told Bird,
"Thank you for returning my joke book.
I will read it today."
"You are a good friend," Bunny added.

SRA Open Court Reading

Who Took My Book?

by Joyce Mallery
illustrated by Deborah Colvin Borgo

SRA
A Division of The McGraw-Hill Companies
Columbus, Ohio

SRA/McGraw-Hill
A Division of The **McGraw-Hill** *Companies*

Printed in the United States of America.

Send all inquiries to:
SRA/McGraw-Hill
8787 Orion Place
Columbus, OH 43240-4027

"This book makes me laugh.
It is funny!" said Bird.
"This joke book was on the path home
from school. But I will give it back."

“I heard a laugh.
Should we look here?” Mom asked.
Mom and Bunny looked behind a wood pile.

SRA
Open Court
Reading

Bunny got home from school.
He shook out his backpack.
“Where is my joke book?” he asked.

“Oh, no! Where is your joke book?” asked Mom. “I will help you look for it.”

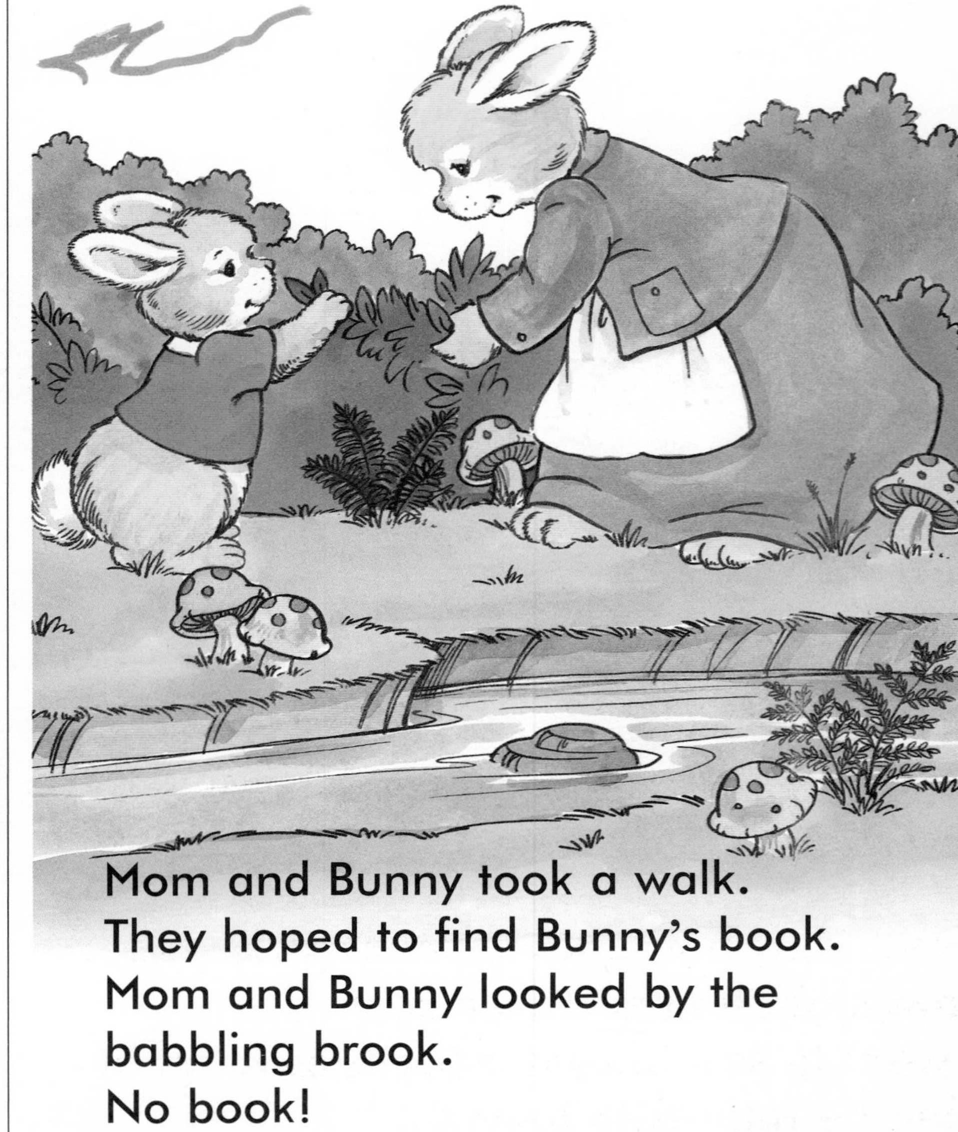

Mom and Bunny took a walk.
They hoped to find Bunny’s book.
Mom and Bunny looked by the babbling brook.
No book!

At the end of his show Chowder tossed flowers from his hat. The crowd clapped and cheered. Then Chowder ran off the stage. The Browns sang silly songs all the way home. They howled with laughter. When the Browns got home, Howie said, "I want to see Chowder the Clown again when he returns to town."

SRA Open Court Reading

A Clown Comes to Town

by Dina McClellan
illustrated by Len Epstein

A Division of The McGraw-Hill Companies
Columbus, Ohio

SRA/McGraw-Hill
A Division of The McGraw-Hill Companies

Printed in the United States of America.

Send all inquiries to:
SRA/McGraw-Hill
8787 Orion Place
Columbus, OH 43240-4027

Then Chowder the Clown came on stage
—and WOW! He was great!
We could not guess how he did his tricks.
He made a dog meow and a cat bow-wow!
He changed a fish into an owl!
He went "Poof!" and a ball became
powder.

Everyone in town was there.
Town Hall was hot and crowded.
Mom and Dad met friends and talked.
Howie was allowed to eat
whatever he liked.

The Browns were not outside that day.
Each person sat by a TV.
“Sunny today, then showers!” a man
on TV said.
“Pow, Pow! To the tower, men!” said
the other box.
Mom, Dad, and Howie wore frowns.
No one had much to say.

Howie shut down his game.
"What is on now?" he asked his dad.
"A woman in a gown has
a gold crown on her head. She is
taking a bow."
Howie made a face.

"This paper says that Chowder
the Clown is now at Town Hall!
How about it? Shall we go?" asked Mom.
"A clown named Chowder?" asked Dad
with a scowl on his brow.
"I'm too old for clowns, Mom!" fussed Howie.
"I'm not!" said Mom.
And that was that. The Browns were off!

Pat went to feed Max.
"Look, Mom!" Pat whispered.
"Max found a friend!"
Max and the mouse were very happy.

SRA Open Court Reading

Max the Grouch

by Joyce Mallery
illustrated by Len Epstein

A Division of The McGraw-Hill Companies
Columbus, Ohio

SRA/McGraw-Hill
A Division of The McGraw-Hill Companies

Printed in the United States of America.

Send all inquiries to:
SRA/McGraw-Hill
8787 Orion Place
Columbus, OH 43240-4027

"How about a long walk?" asked Pat.
She and Max walked for an hour.
Now Max was a tired grouch.

Max put a bone in his mouth.
Then he spit it out and made a loud sound!
Dog bones did not help.
Max was still a grouch.

SRA
Open Court
Reading

Pat loved her brown and
white hound named Max.
But Max was a grouch!

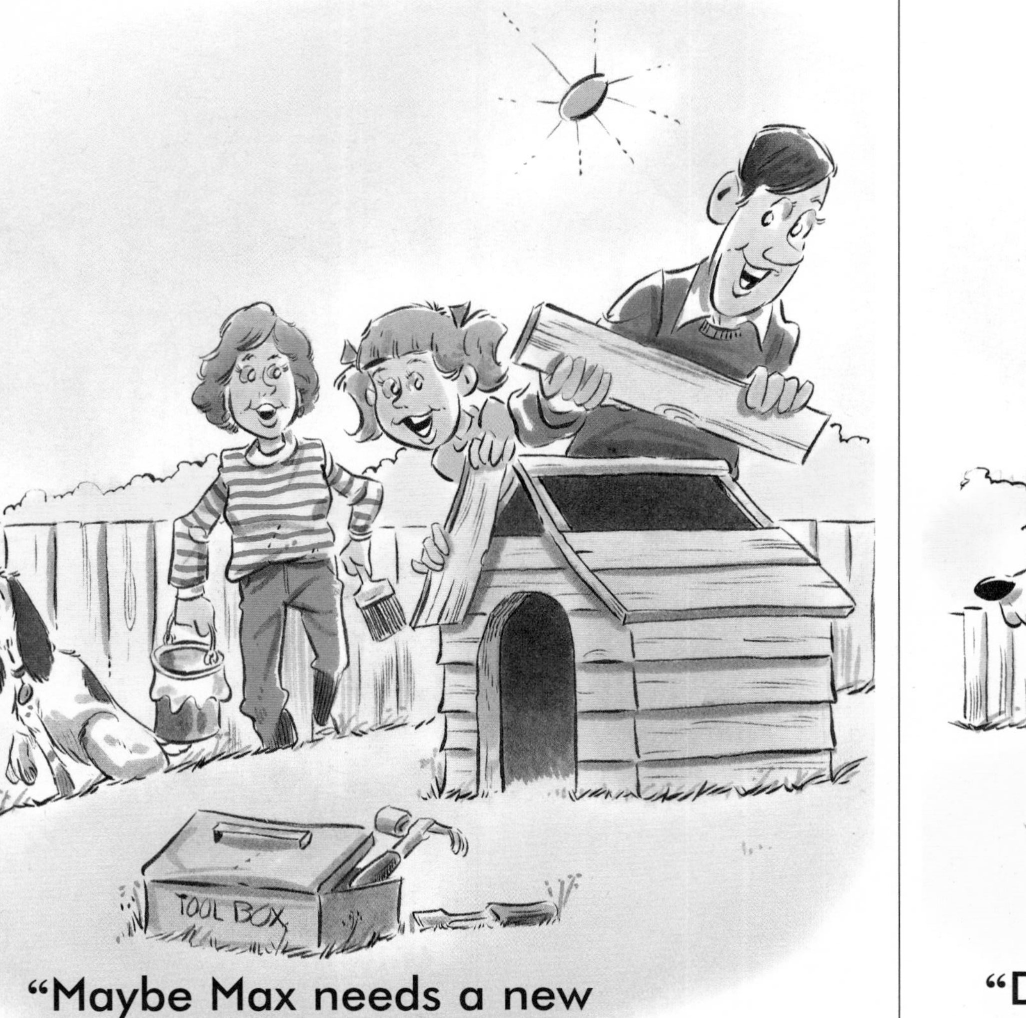

"Maybe Max needs a new dog house," said Mom. But Max was still a grouch.

"Does he want a pound of dog bones?" asked Dad. Dad put a large bone on the ground.

In winter the garden is frozen.
Flowers are waiting under the ground.
Next spring, the garden will bloom
and be new again.

Open Court Reading

Our Town Garden

by Rebecca Blankenhorn
illustrated by Susanne DeMarco

A Division of The McGraw-Hill Companies
Columbus, Ohio

SRA/McGraw-Hill
A Division of The McGraw-Hill Companies

Printed in the United States of America.

Send all inquiries to:
SRA/McGraw-Hill
8787 Orion Place
Columbus, OH 43240-4027

When fall comes, the leaves fall.
The frost makes our plants turn brown.
It's time for us to take the old plants out of the ground. Then we hang up bird feeders.

We have a picnic at the town park.
We play tag and shout.
We play until the sun goes down.

Open Court Reading

Planting Time

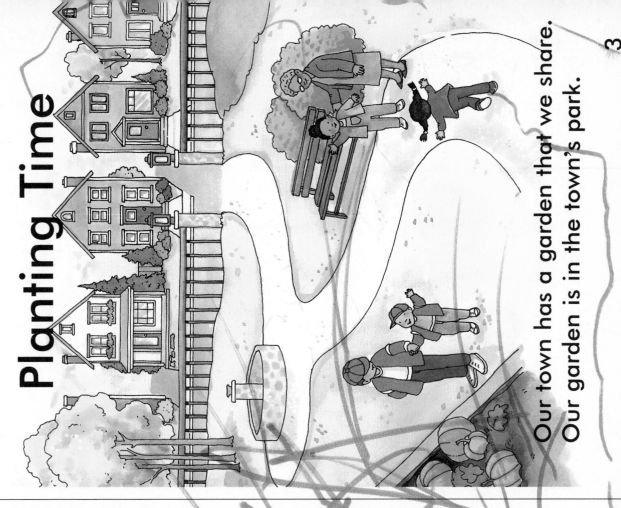

Our town has a garden that we share.
Our garden is in the town's park.

We plow and rake the ground.
We take out large sticks and stones.
Then we plan the garden.

Our crew works for hours!
Then we are surrounded by pounds
and pounds of super cucumbers,
beans, peas, and tomatoes.

At the end of summer, we harvest the food that we planted and grew.

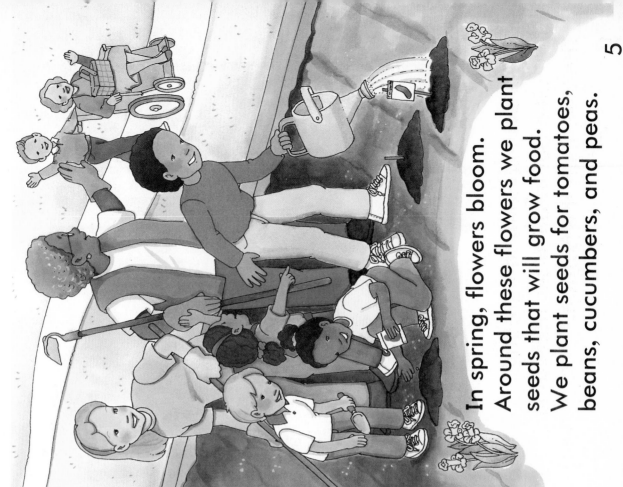

In spring, flowers bloom. Around these flowers we plant seeds that will grow food. We plant seeds for tomatoes, beans, cucumbers, and peas.

If we could look underground,
we could see how seeds sprout.
Sprouts drink water from the ground.

We take good care of the ground
around the plants.
We take out the weeds.
Plants are stronger when they are not
crowded by weeds.

SRA Open Court Reading

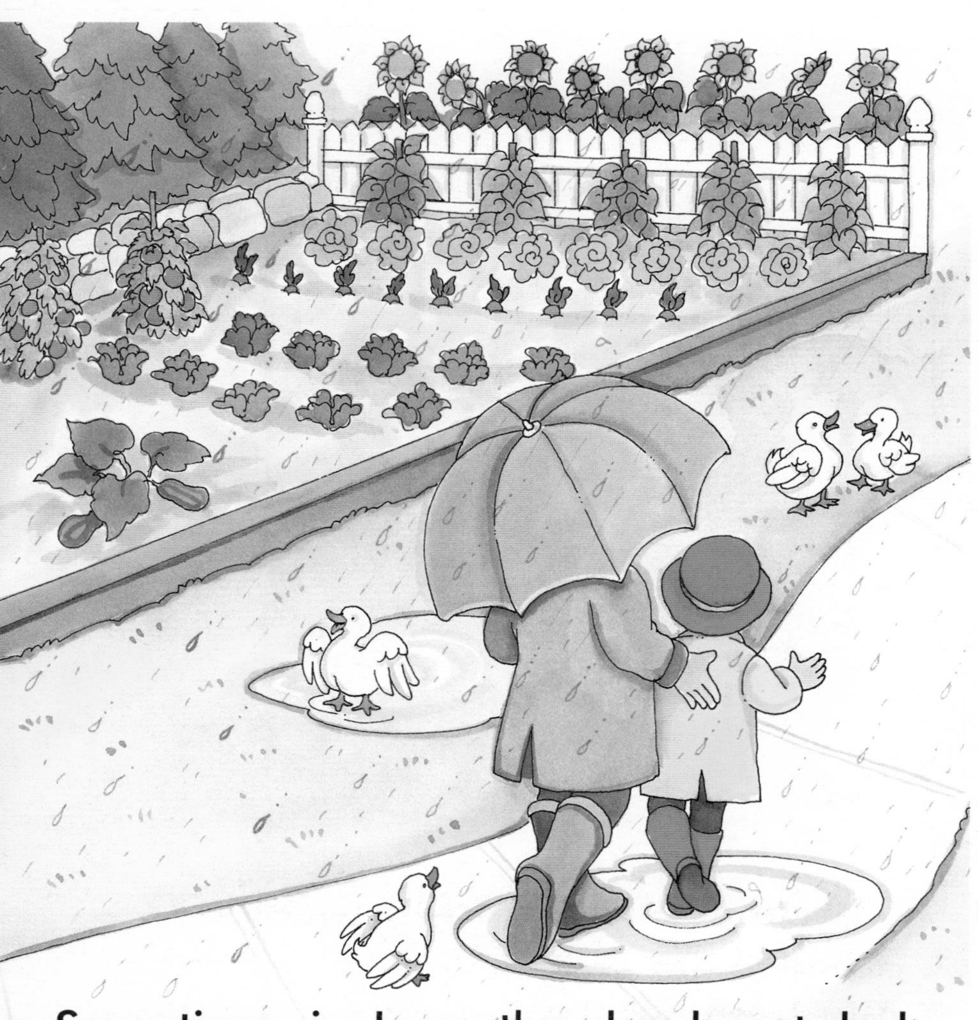

Sometimes in June, the clouds get dark.
We hear loud thunder.
Then the garden gets a shower!

Worms and ants dig holes that
make the ground better for the plants.
These holes let air into the ground.

Sunflowers are gold and brown.
Sunflowers tower over the fence
in summer.
Butterflies and bees swoop around
the garden.

The Harvest

Everyone visits the town square in
summer.
Children play all around.
We work in the garden.
But no dogs are allowed!

“Perhaps I don’t really want crabs at all…” said Sailor Paul.

Open Court Reading

Sailor Paul and the Crabs

by Tim Paulson
illustrated by Jan Pyk

SRA
A Division of The McGraw-Hill Companies
Columbus, Ohio

SRA/McGraw-Hill
A Division of The **McGraw-Hill** *Companies*

Printed in the United States of America.

Send all inquiries to:
SRA/McGraw-Hill
8787 Orion Place
Columbus, OH 43240-4027

"I'll catch some crabs if it's the last thing I do," said Sailor Paul. When rain began falling, Sailor Paul put an awning on his deck. When a cold wind blew, he put on a shawl. The sea became wild and awful, but Paul would not quit. At last, his nets were full, and Paul began pulling and pulling.

When his nets were full again, Paul pulled them quickly in. "I'm fishing for crabs, not shark!" yelled Sailor Paul. "Get off my deck if you don't want a brawl!" Sailor Paul fished and fished. He netted ten tuna, five whales, and a hundred prawns. But he did not catch one crab.

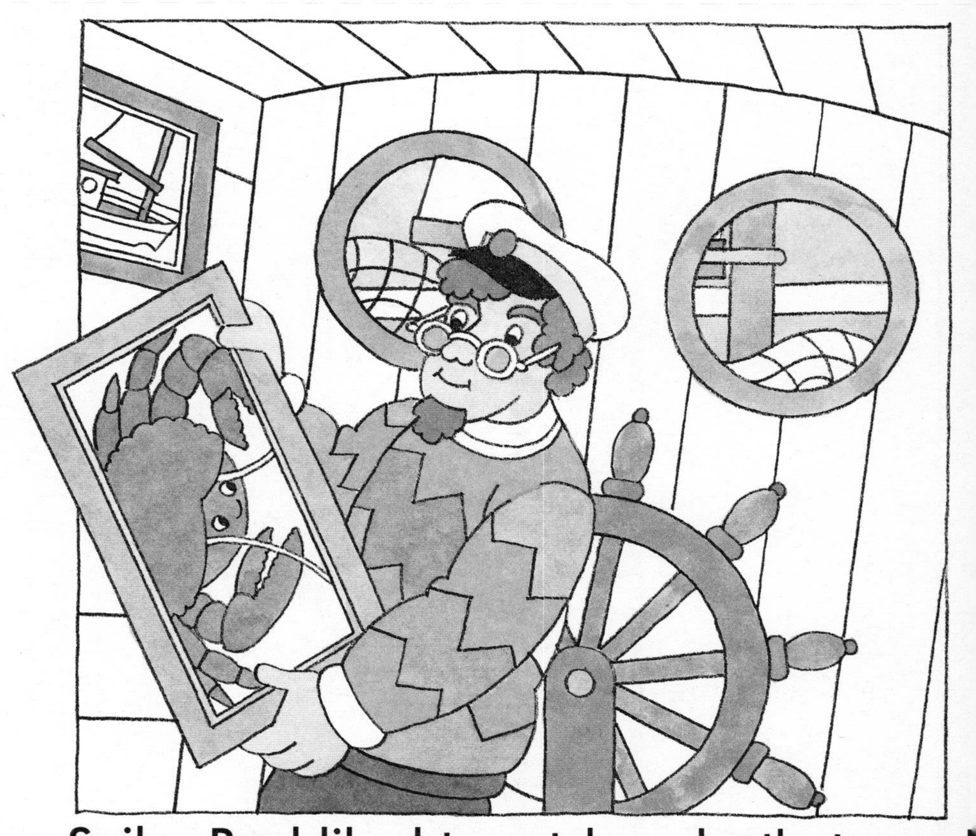

Sailor Paul liked to catch crabs that crawl in the sea. Paul went out in his yawl. It was a small fishing boat named Awful Annie. He caught crabs in big nets and then hauled in his catch. But he never trapped a single crab.

With a big yawn he set out to sea at dawn. "I'm going to catch a crab today!" yelled Sailor Paul. Soon his nets were full and taut, and Paul hauled them up on deck.

"Get away, silly squid," scolded Sailor Paul. "Don't sprawl on my yawl. I catch crabs, not squid."

King Knox's knight packed a knapsack.
He left and lived on a farm.
He was happy from that day on.

SRA Open Court Reading

The Knight Who Did Not Know

by Joyce Mallery
illustrated by Len Epstein

SRA
A Division of The McGraw-Hill Companies
Columbus, Ohio

SRA/McGraw-Hill

A Division of The **McGraw-Hill** *Companies*

Printed in the United States of America.

Send all inquiries to:
SRA/McGraw-Hill
8787 Orion Place
Columbus, OH 43240-4027

His knight got down on his knees.
"I know one thing," he replied.
"I don't want to be a knight any more!"

King Knox was getting mad.
He knocked on the knight's door.
"When I ask you to do something,
you say you don't know how.
What **do** you know?"

SRA Open Court Reading

Long ago, King Knox had a knight that lived with him.
King Knox asked his knight to do many things.
"Can you tie this knot?" asked King Knox
"I don't know how," replied his knight.

"Can you sharpen this knife?" asked King Knox.

"I don't know how," replied his knight, "but this knife would be good to butter my roll."

"Can you knit some socks for me?" asked King Knox.

"No, I don't know how," replied his knight, "but this wool would make a nice, soft bed."

"Stop that noise!" yelled Big Boy.
"I want to sleep!"
Big Boy got the point.
He never howled at Roy again.

SRA Open Court Reading

Roy and Big Boy

by Joyce Mallery
illustrated by Jan Pyk

A Division of The McGraw-Hill Companies
Columbus, Ohio

SRA/McGraw-Hill
A Division of The McGraw-Hill Companies

Printed in the United States of America.

Send all inquiries to:
SRA/McGraw-Hill
8787 Orion Place
Columbus, OH 43240-4027

Next day Rooster woke all the farm animals.
Big Boy was still sleeping in the barn.
Dog started howling, and all the animals joined in!

"You are my loyal friends," oinked Roy.
"You can help me with my plan."

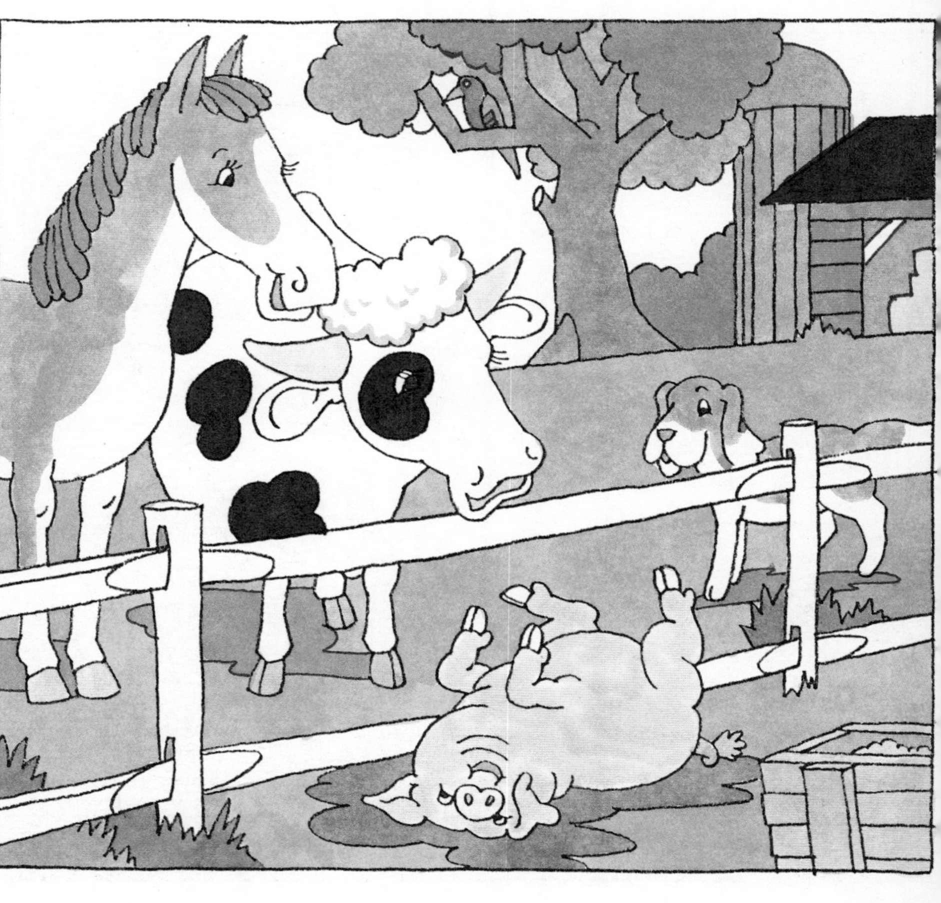

Roy was a pig who lived on a big farm. He enjoyed eating and rolling in muddy soil all day long.

But the cat, Big Boy, could spoil his day.
That cat loved to annoy Roy by howling.

"Just avoid him," Cow told Roy.
"We should put him in oil," said Dog.
"That cat is spoiled."

“We were wrong,” said Little Wren.
“It is a tool to fix things.”
“You are a smart bird,” Dad told Little Wren.

Open Court Reading

Little Wren’s Surprise

by Joyce Mallery
illustrated by Deborah Colvin Borgo

SRA
A Division of The McGraw-Hill Companies
Columbus, Ohio

SRA/McGraw-Hill
A Division of The McGraw-Hill Companies

Printed in the United States of America.

Send all inquiries to:
SRA/McGraw-Hill
8787 Orion Place
Columbus, OH 43240-4027

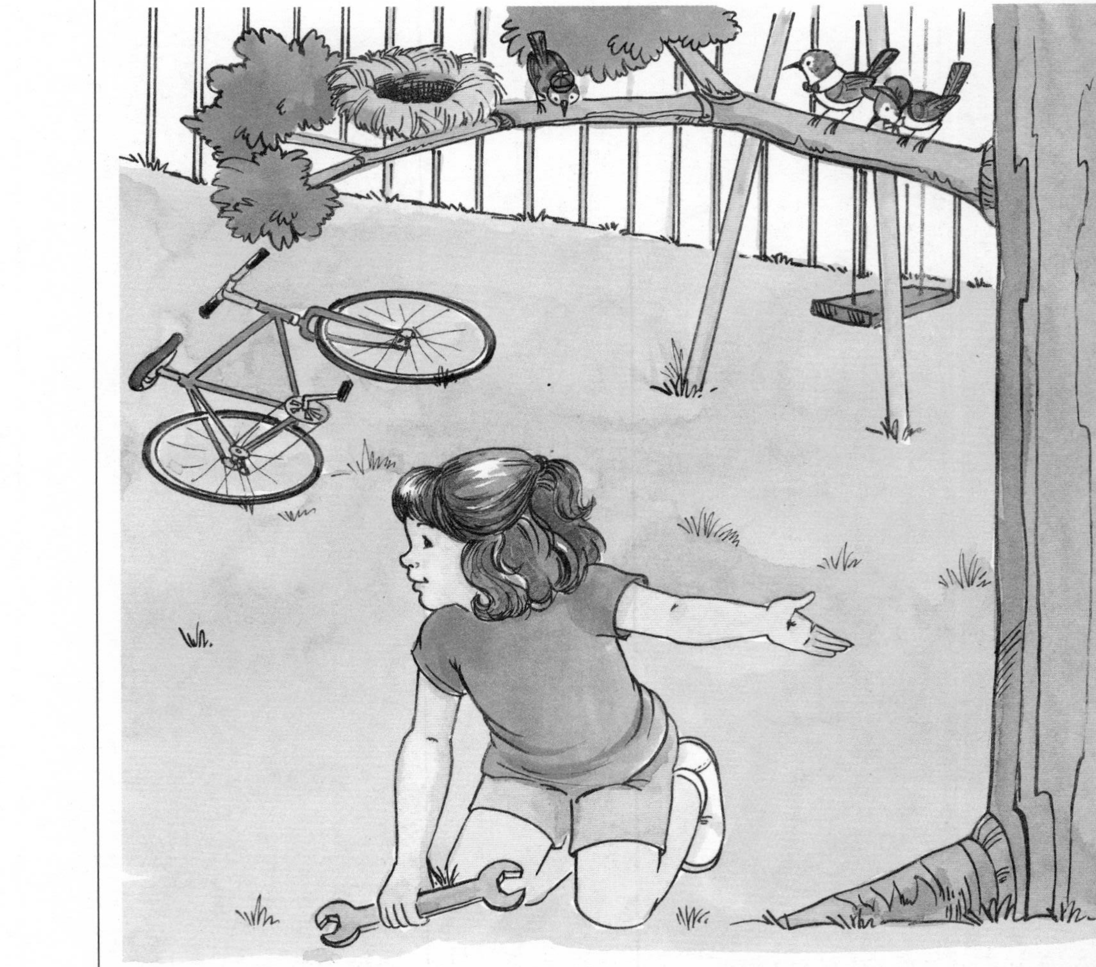

Little Wren watched a girl come into the yard. “Here’s that missing wrench, Ben,” she yelled. “Now we can fix my bike.”

"Will it hurt us?" asked Little Wren.
"Let's wrap it up."
But the paper had a big wrinkle.
It did not fit.

A wren family lived in a nest in an oak tree. One day they found a strange thing on the ground.

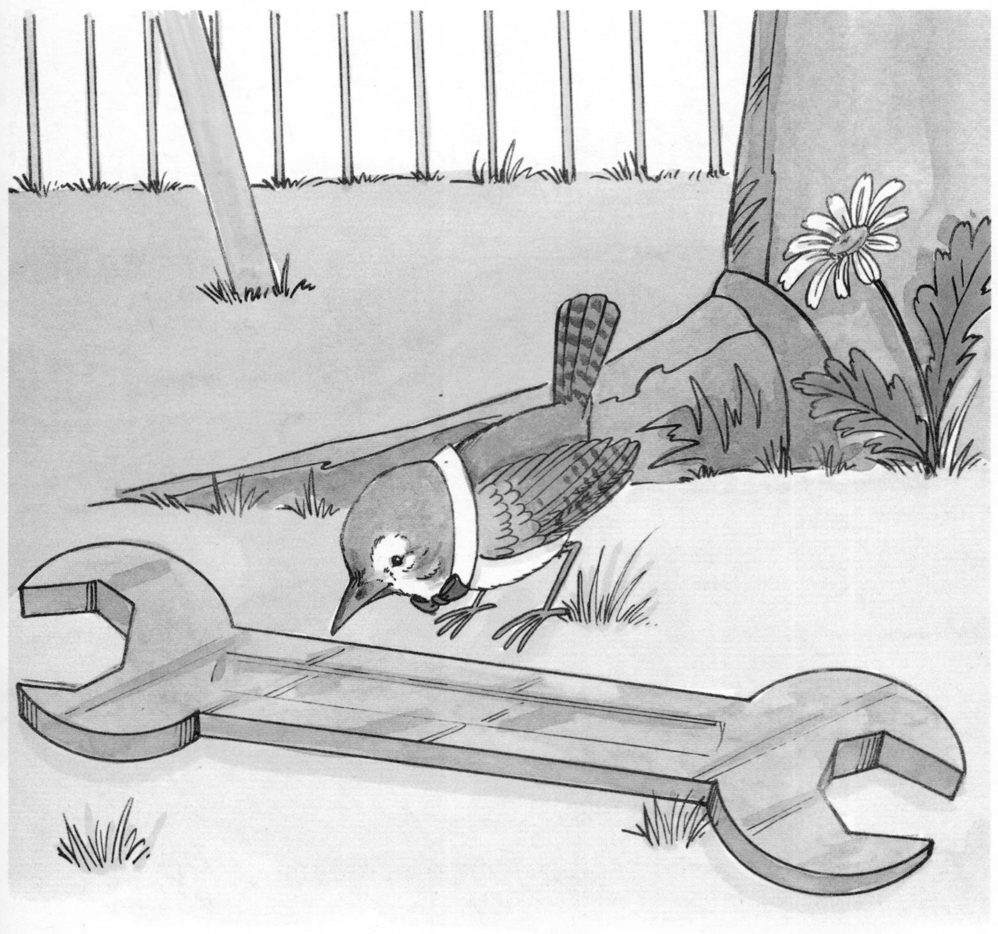

"What could it be?" asked Dad. He tried wriggling under it, but it was too big.

"Can you write with it?" asked Mom. Mom rubbed the side with a leaf. But it didn't make a mark.

Phil phoned Fred. "Please come to my place!" he said. "I have a yip yap, zig zag surprise for you! And it barks!"

Open Court Reading

A Photo for Fred

by Marilee Robin Burton
illustrated by Meryl Henderson

A Division of The McGraw-Hill Companies
Columbus, Ohio

SRA/McGraw-Hill

A Division of The **McGraw-Hill** *Companies*

Printed in the United States of America.

Send all inquiries to:
SRA/McGraw-Hill
8787 Orion Place
Columbus, OH 43240-4027

"Phooey!" grumbled Phil. "No photo for Fred! My pup is in a yip yap, zig zag stage! A photo is not the best way to see him!"

"I will take his photo!" said Phil.
He took Ralph home. Phil's pup barked,
wagged, zigged, and zagged.
He yipped, yapped, and romped.

SRA Open Court Reading

Phil got a pet puppy. He named his puppy Ralph. Phil wanted his friend Fred to see Ralph. Phil planned on sending Fred a photo of Ralph.

Phil took Ralph to a photo shop.
He asked for a photo shot.
Ralph did not sit still. He barked and wagged and zigged and zagged.

Ralph's photo was a blur.
"Phooey!" muttered Phil. "This is a phony photo of my pet pup.
Ralph looks like a funny pheasant!"

Fran and I walked home.
We talked about our old schools.
I had a new friend.
That first day was not so awful after all.

Open Court Reading

Patty's Awful Day

by Laura Kirsch
illustrated by Kersti Frigell

SRA
A Division of The McGraw-Hill Companies
Columbus, Ohio

SRA/McGraw-Hill
A Division of The **McGraw-Hill** *Companies*

Printed in the United States of America.

Send all inquiries to:
SRA/McGraw-Hill
8787 Orion Place
Columbus, OH 43240-4027

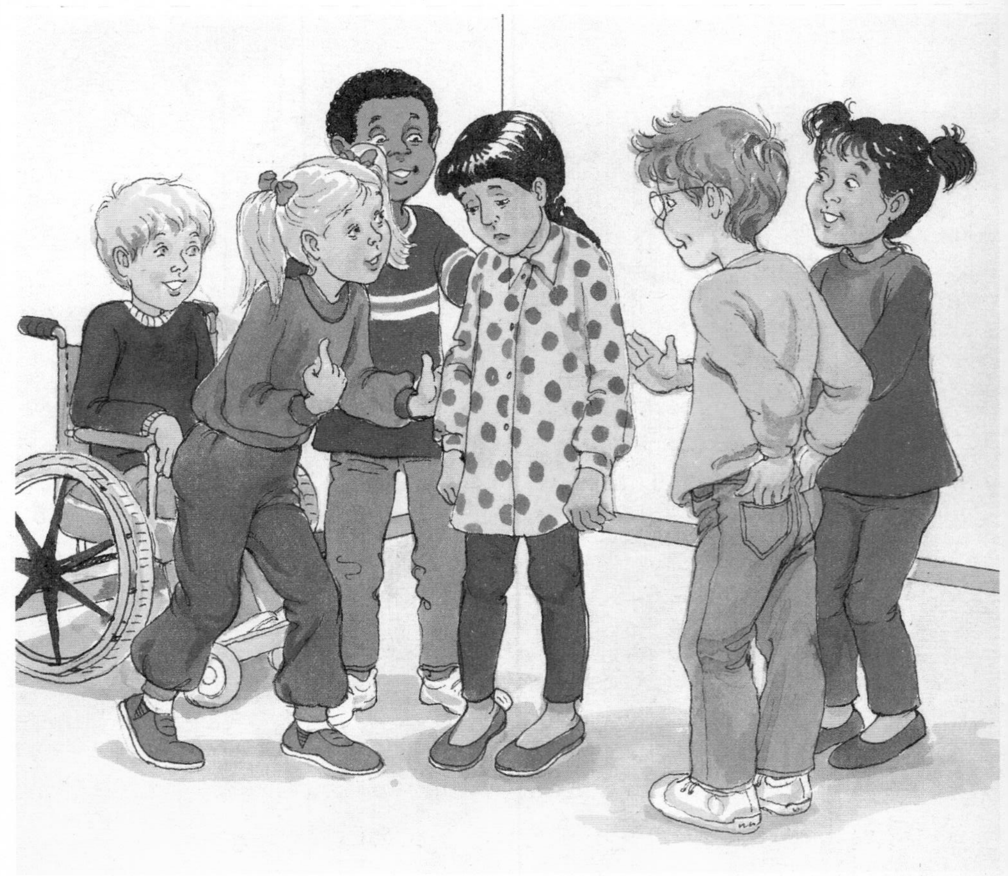

"I know how you feel," said Fran.
"I came here last month.
It is fun now.
You will make new friends.
I'll be your first."

"This is my old class," I explained.
"We played kickball at recess.
We were the champions.
We had Show and Tell, too.
I miss my old friends and my teacher."

I felt awful.

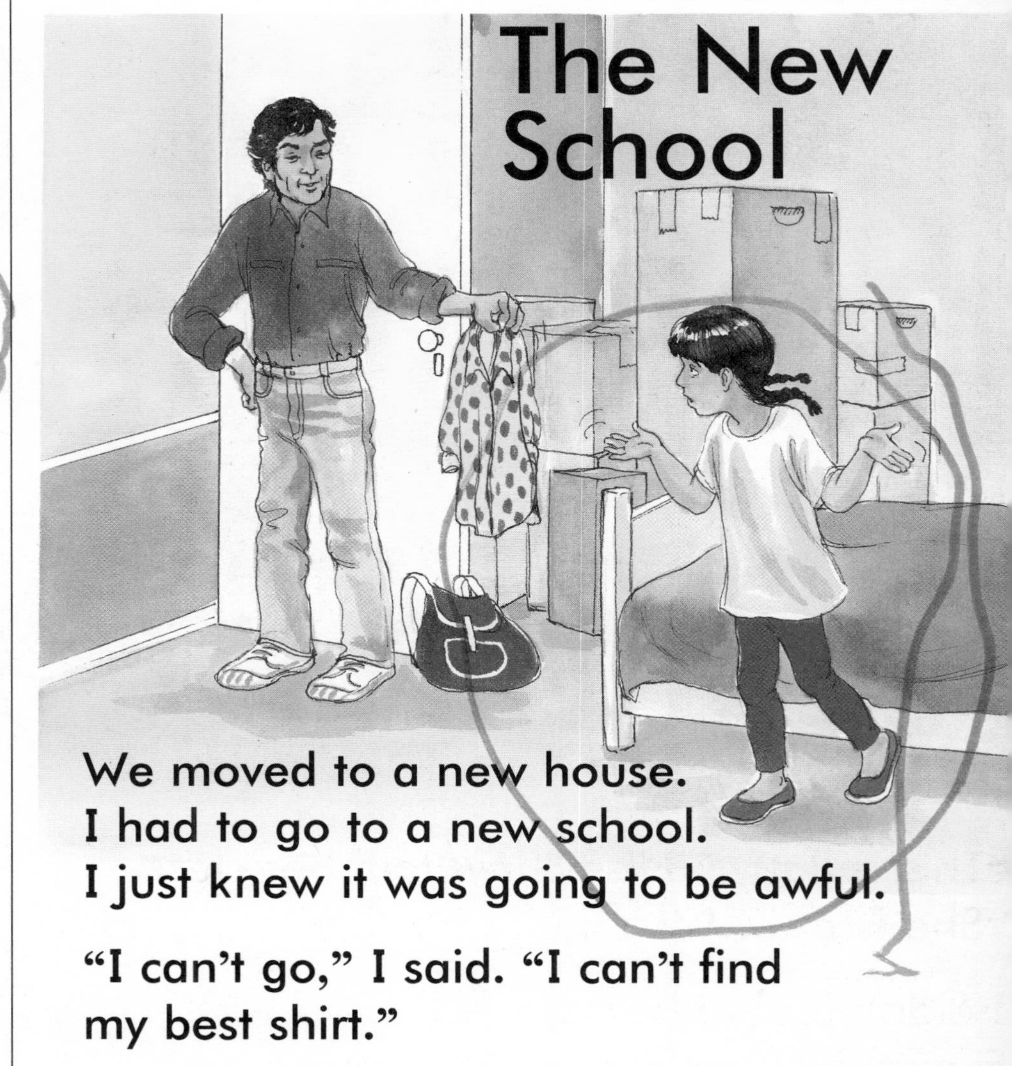

The New School

We moved to a new house.
I had to go to a new school.
I just knew it was going to be awful.

"I can't go," I said. "I can't find my best shirt."

"That's silly," said Dad. "Here's a shirt. Now hurry, or you will be late."

"This is Patty," Miss Shaw told her class.
"She is new. Let's make her feel at home."

I didn't feel at home.
Everything was wrong. I felt awful.
I missed my old school.

Then Miss Shaw asked me to tell
about my old school.
I showed them my drawing.
I told the class about my friends.

I didn't have anything for Show and Tell.
My coin collection and a hat Mom helped me knit were still packed in boxes at home.
Everyone had neat things.
Sandy had a new camera.
She took our photo.

"See my cartoon lunch box, Patty.
Cartoons are cool," stated Sandy.

My lunch box has whales.
All my old friends had animal lunch boxes.

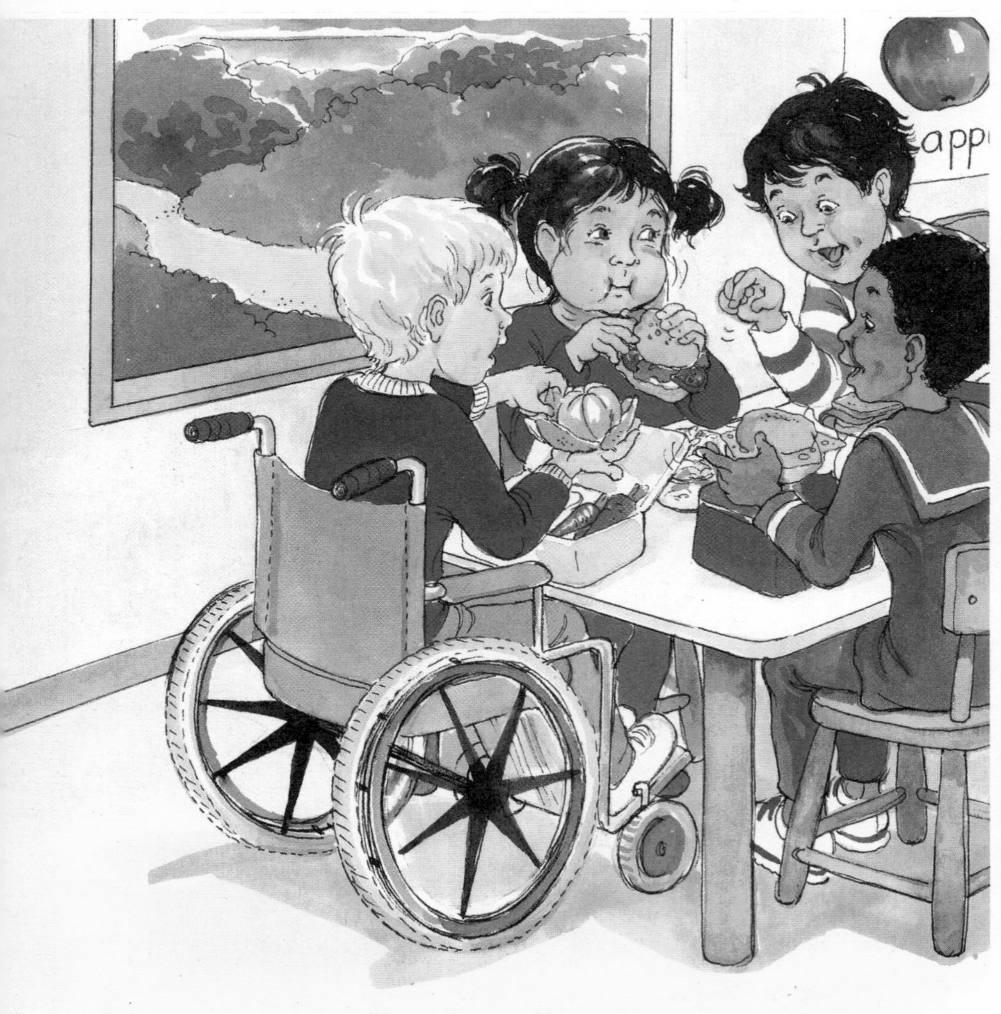

“I keep my crayons sharp,” Sandy told Patty.
“I enjoy neat drawings.”

I felt awful. I wanted to crawl home.

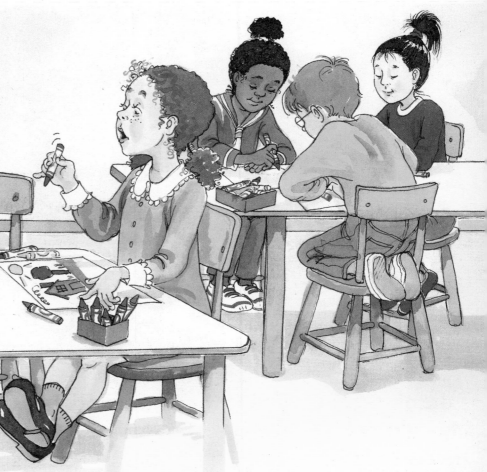

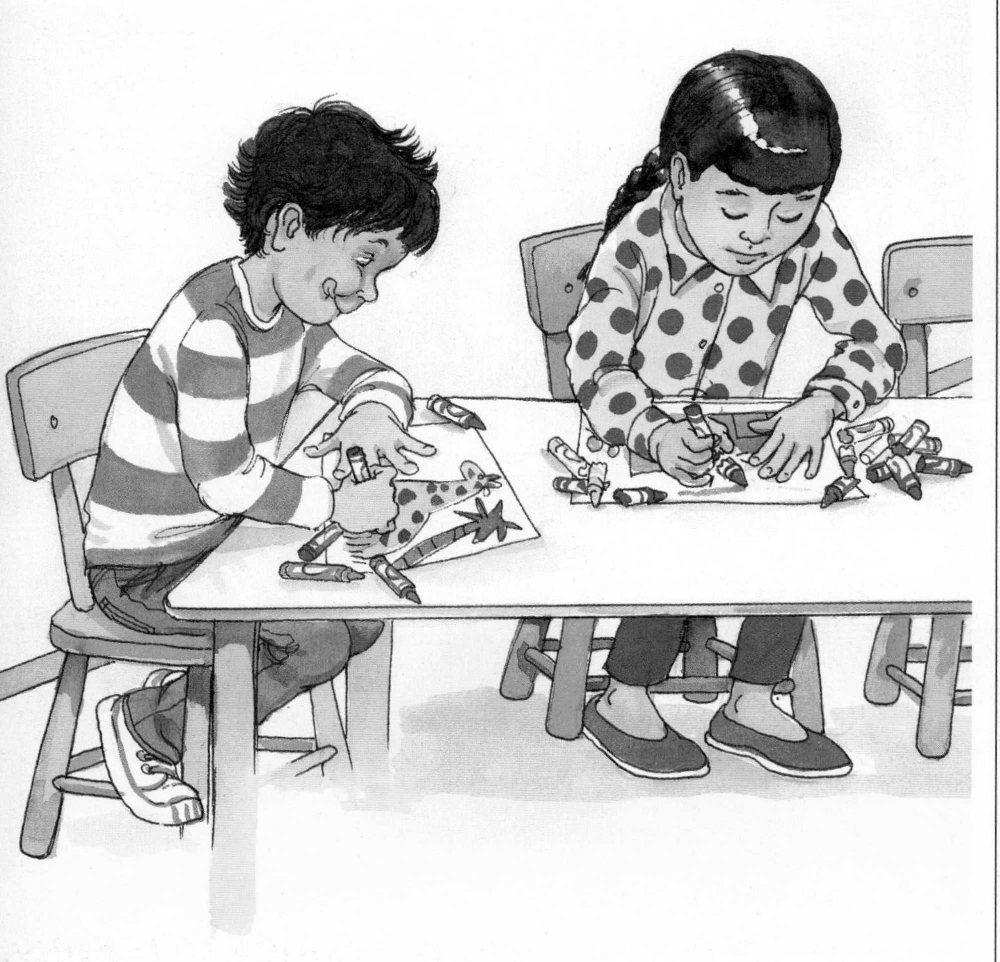

Miss Shaw told us to draw.
I drew my old school and my friends.
All my crayons broke.

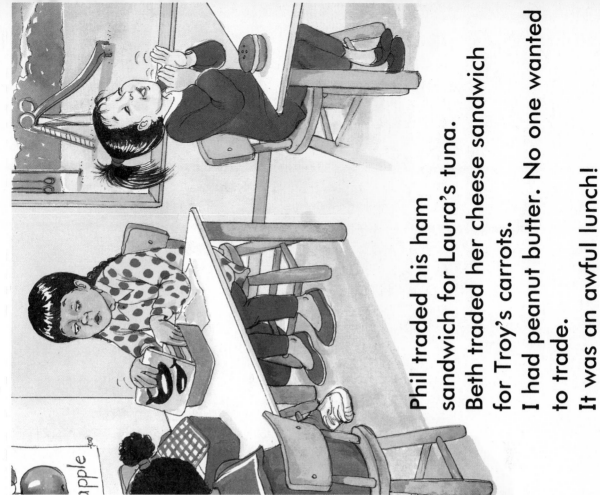

Phil traded his ham sandwich for Laura's tuna.
Beth traded her cheese sandwich for Troy's carrots.
I had peanut butter. No one wanted to trade.
It was an awful lunch!

A New Friend

Even recess was awful!
I was the last one picked to join the team.
Just when it was my turn, the bell rang.
I didn't get to show them what a good player I am.

"Welcome to the Everybody Club!"
called Rose.

Open Court Reading

The Everybody Club

by Anne O'Brien
illustrated by Gioia Fiammenghi

A Division of The McGraw-Hill Companies
Columbus, Ohio

SRA/McGraw-Hill
A Division of The McGraw-Hill Companies

Printed in the United States of America.

Send all inquiries to:
SRA/McGraw-Hill
8787 Orion Place
Columbus, OH 43240-4027

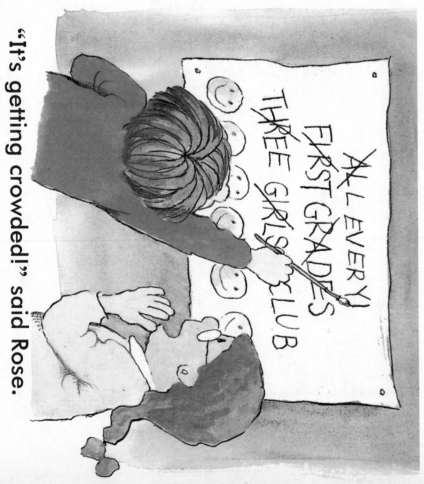

"It's getting crowded!" said Rose.
"How about just calling it
the Everybody Club?"
Abby crossed out All Grades
and painted Everybody.
Then she painted lots of faces.

"Hi!" called Abby's little sister.
"Can I come up?"
"Well," said Abby, "we have a club.
It's called the All Grades Club,
and you aren't even in kindergarten!"

The Girls Club

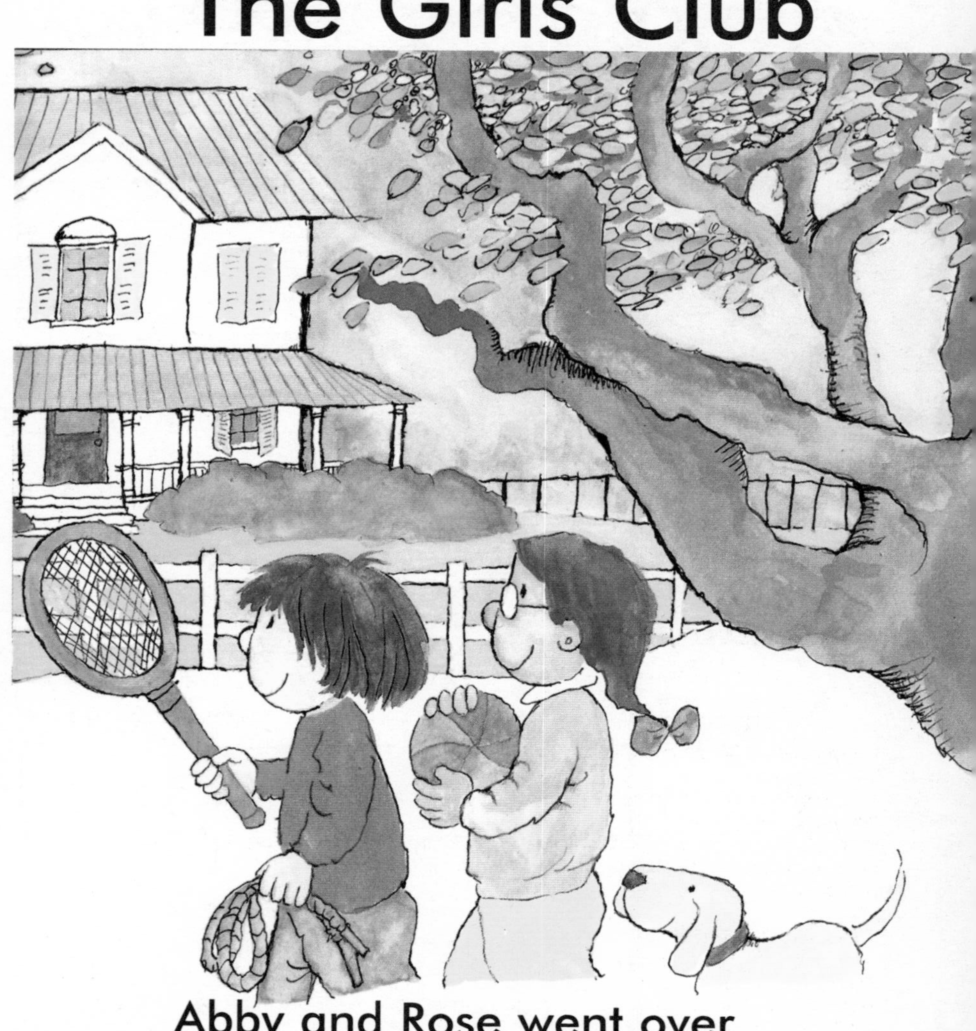

Abby and Rose went over
to Nancy's yard to play.

"Hurry up!" called Nancy.
"We can play in my tree house!"

"Well," said Holly,
"how about the All Grades Club?"
Abby crossed out First,
added an s, and painted All.
Then she painted a sixth face.
"Now we are the All Grades Club!"
chuckled Rose.

"Hi!" called Nancy's big brother, Tom.
"Can I climb up?"
"Well," said Nancy, "this is
the First Grade Club,
and you aren't in first grade."
Tom scowled.

"Wow! What a neat place!" said Abby.
"Let's make a club!" said Rose.
"We can call it the Three Girls Club."

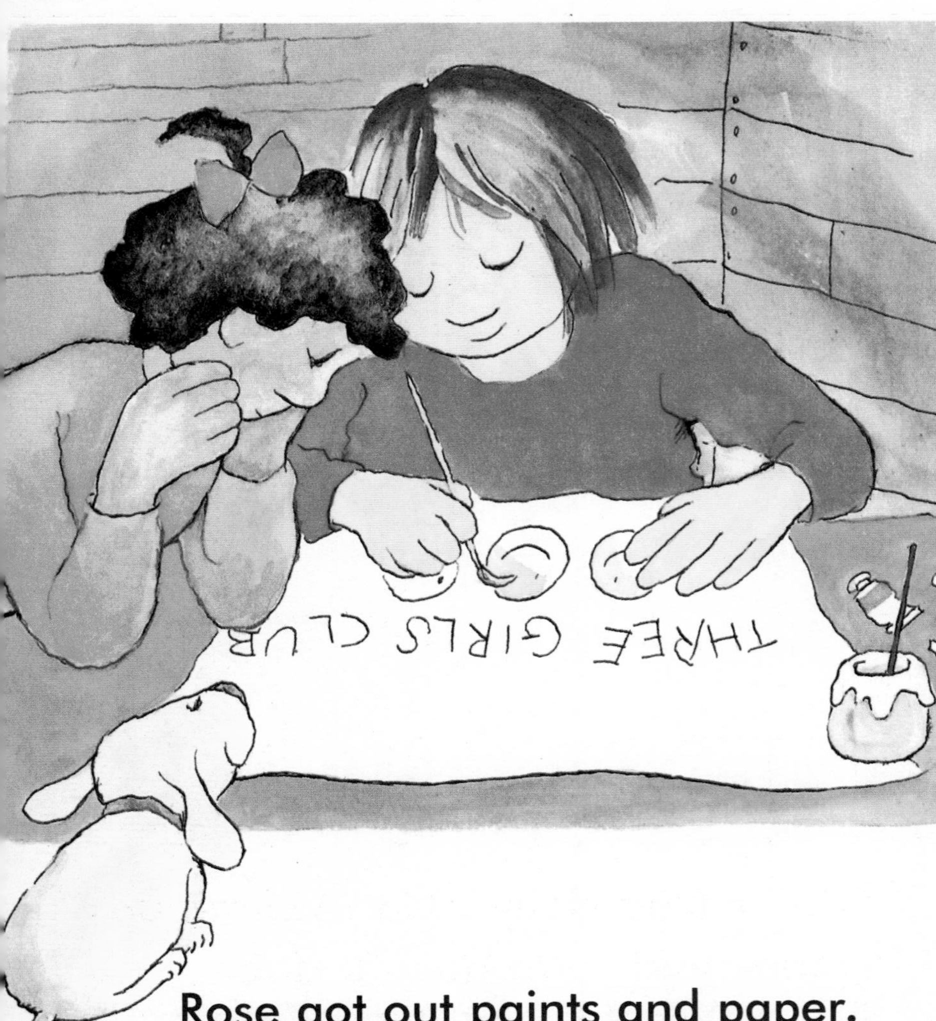

Rose got out paints and paper.
Abby painted Three Girls Club
and three faces on the paper.

"Well," said Nancy,
"how about the First Grade Club?"
Abby crossed out Girls and painted
First Grade. Then she painted a fifth
face.
"Now we are the First Grade Club!"
said Rose.

The Everybody Club

"Hi!" called David. "Can I climb up?"
"Well," said Rose, "this is a club for girls, and you aren't a girl."
David frowned. He kicked the dirt.

"Hi!" called Holly. "Can I climb up?"
Nancy said, "We have a club.
It's called Three Girls Club.
You would make four."
Holly looked down. She hung her head.

"Well," said Nancy,
"how about just Girls Club?"
Abby crossed out <u>Three</u>
and painted a face.
"Now we are the Girls Club!"
shouted Rose.

Lenny picked up the bunny.
He put it back in the crib.
The baby stopped crying.
"Superhero to the rescue,"
Lenny whispered.

Open Court Reading

Superhero to the Rescue

by Anne O'Brien
illustrated by Meg McLean

A Division of The McGraw-Hill Companies
Columbus, Ohio

SRA/McGraw-Hill
A Division of The McGraw-Hill Companies

Printed in the United States of America.

Send all inquiries to:
SRA/McGraw-Hill
8787 Orion Place
Columbus, OH 43240-4027

Lenny went upstairs.
The baby was crying.
His bunny had fallen out of his crib.

At naptime Lenny became bored.
His mom had put Jenny
and the baby down for naps.

The Cape

Lenny wanted to be a superhero.

Lenny put on his cape.
"Superhero to the rescue!" he shouted.
He raced downstairs.

Lenny's mom found him in the tree.
She helped him get down.
"Play safer," she said.
They went back inside.

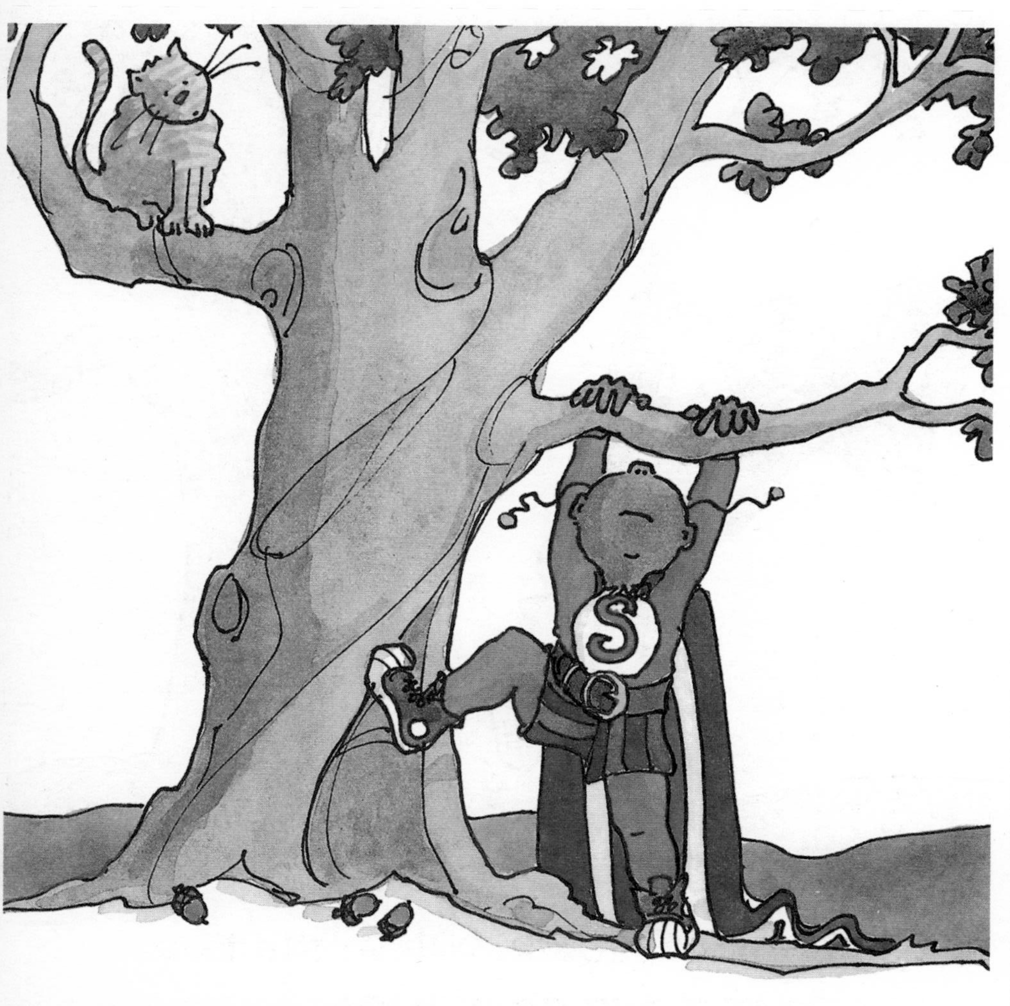

"Superhero to the rescue!"
shouted Lenny.
He reached for a branch.

Lenny landed on top
of his little sister Jenny.
"Ouch!" shouted Jenny.
She began crying.

"Go play quietly,"
Lenny's mom told him.

"Pow! Wow!" shouted Lenny.
He raced to an oak tree.
Lenny's cat sat on one branch.
"Meow!" cried his cat.

Lenny to the Rescue

"Play something quieter,"
Lenny's mom told him.
Lenny went outside.

Lenny and Jenny played house with the baby.
Jenny grabbed the baby's doll.

"Superhero is here!"
shouted Lenny.
He pushed Jenny out of the way.

Jenny and the baby
both began crying.

Andy was an artist.
His glass made rainbows dance in rooms.
It also made him brave.

Open Court Reading

Mr. Lee

by Jennifer Jacobson
illustrated by Jon Agee

A Division of The McGraw-Hill Companies
Columbus, Ohio

SRA/McGraw-Hill
A Division of The ***McGraw-Hill*** *Companies*

Printed in the United States of America.

Send all inquiries to:
SRA/McGraw-Hill
8787 Orion Place
Columbus, OH 43240-4027

Andy turned around.
The chair was not knocking and
drapes were not swaying.
The tablecloth was not floating.
The hat was not tipping.
It was not dark and scary in there.
Rainbows danced in the room.

Andy felt a breeze.
He found a broken window.
He put in the new window.
It fit perfectly.

SRA
Open Court Reading

Mr. Lee the Timid

Mr. Andy Lee was a timid man.
He was also an artist and
made stained glass windows.
His glass made rainbows dance in rooms.

One day, Andy made
a window pane for an inn.
He took the window pane to an inn
that was far away.
Timid Andy walked and walked.

Timid Andy walked in.
It was dark and scary.
A chair was knocking,
drapes were swaying,
a tablecloth was floating,
a hat was tipping.

5

12

Andy came to the town where
the inn was.
Down the street ran a maid.
"Turn back!" she cried.
"Do not go!
A chair is knocking.
Drapes are swaying.
It's dark and awful in that inn!"

"Stay with me," whispered timid Andy.
"We will go together."

Mr. Lee the Brave

Mr. Lee, the maid, and the cook
stood at the front door.
Out ran an innkeeper.
"Turn back!" she cried.
"A chair is knocking.
Drapes are swaying.
A tablecloth is floating,
and a hat is tipping.
It's dark and scary in here!"

"But what about the window?"
asked Andy.
"I am a timid man,
but this is my best window ever.
I will still put in my window."

Andy and the maid came to a gate.
Out ran a cook waving a spoon.
"Turn back!" cried the cook.
"A chair is knocking.
Drapes are swaying.
A tablecloth is floating.
It's dark and scary in here!"

"Stay with me," said timid Andy.
"We will go together."

Then the real princess ordered her royal sister to take the marbles, the wrench, the toy truck, Cuddles, and the sneakers out from under her royal mattress.

SRA Open Court Reading

Princess Julia

by Patricia Griffith
illustrated by Pat Doyle

SRA
A Division of The McGraw-Hill Companies
Columbus, Ohio

SRA/McGraw-Hill
A Division of The **McGraw-Hill** *Companies*

Printed in the United States of America.

Send all inquiries to:
SRA/McGraw-Hill
8787 Orion Place
Columbus, OH 43240-4027

Julie put on her wrinkled crown.
“That was only a fairy tale,” she cried.
“A real princess can sleep
any place, any time,
any way she wants!
And I am a real princess!”

The next day, Julie looked for her crown.
I picked up her mattress.
"See?" I shouted.
"You are not a real princess!
Remember <u>The Princess and the Pea</u>?
Look under your bed!
No real princess could sleep on all that!"

Julia the Royal

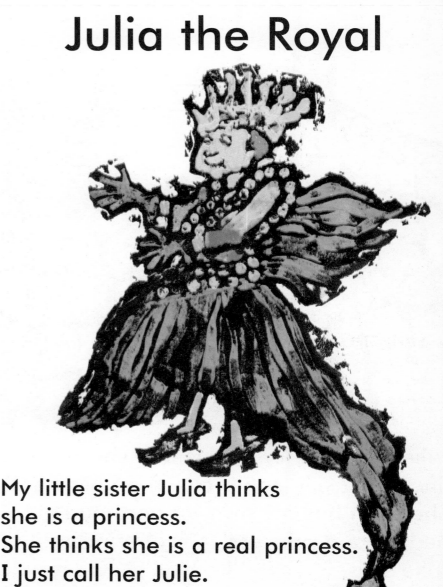

My little sister Julia thinks
she is a princess.
She thinks she is a real princess.
I just call her Julie.

Julie wears fancy gowns and shoes. She has a silly paper crown on her head. She even has a crown on her head in bed! “I’m a princess! A real princess!” Julie says.

The night after that, I put a bag of marbles, a wrench, a toy truck, her bear Cuddles, my old sneakers, and Julie’s own crown under her mattress. Julie never even missed Cuddles!

I tell Julie she is wrong.
Julie tells me that rude sisters
should bow and beg her royal pardon.

One night Dad read us a fairy tale.
He read <u>The Princess and the Pea</u>.
In it, a queen tested a visitor.
The visitor said she was a real princess.
The queen put a pea in a bed.
The visitor tried to sleep on that bed.

The night after that, I put a bag of marbles, a wrench, and a toy truck under Julie's mattress.
Julie never even wiggled.

The visitor could not sleep.
She felt something hard in her bed.
Only a real princess could have felt a single pea in such a bed!

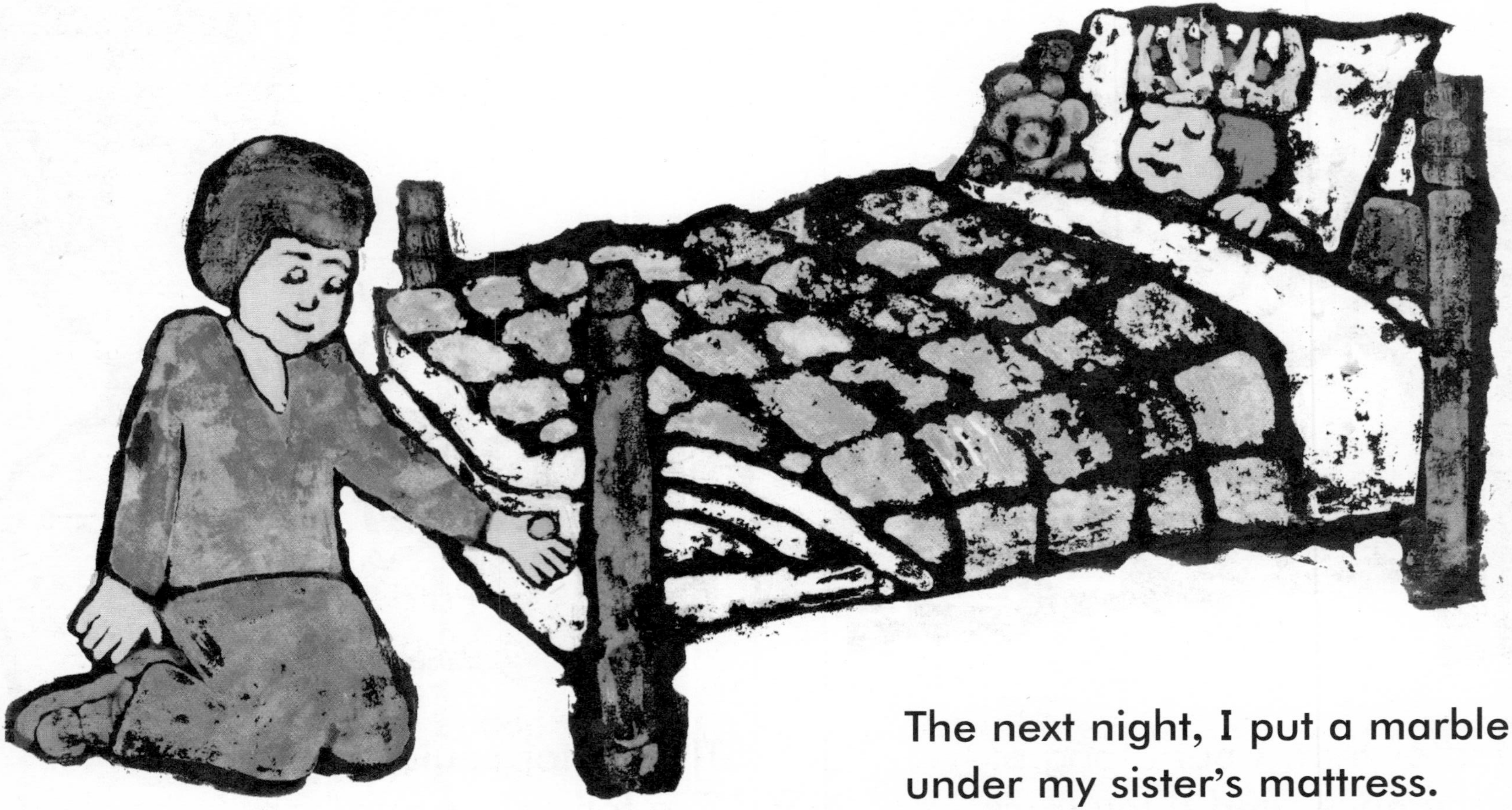

That story of the princess and the pea gave me an idea.

The Test

The next night, I put a marble under my sister's mattress. She never felt a tickle. She slept like a baby all night.

Rabbit giggled and scampered away.
He had tricked a mighty tiger!

Open Court Reading

How the Rabbit Caught the Tiger

by Patricia Griffith
illustrated by Pat Doyle

A Division of The McGraw-Hill Companies
Columbus, Ohio

SRA/McGraw-Hill
A Division of The McGraw-Hill Companies

Printed in the United States of America.

Send all inquiries to:
SRA/McGraw-Hill
8787 Orion Place
Columbus, OH 43240-4027

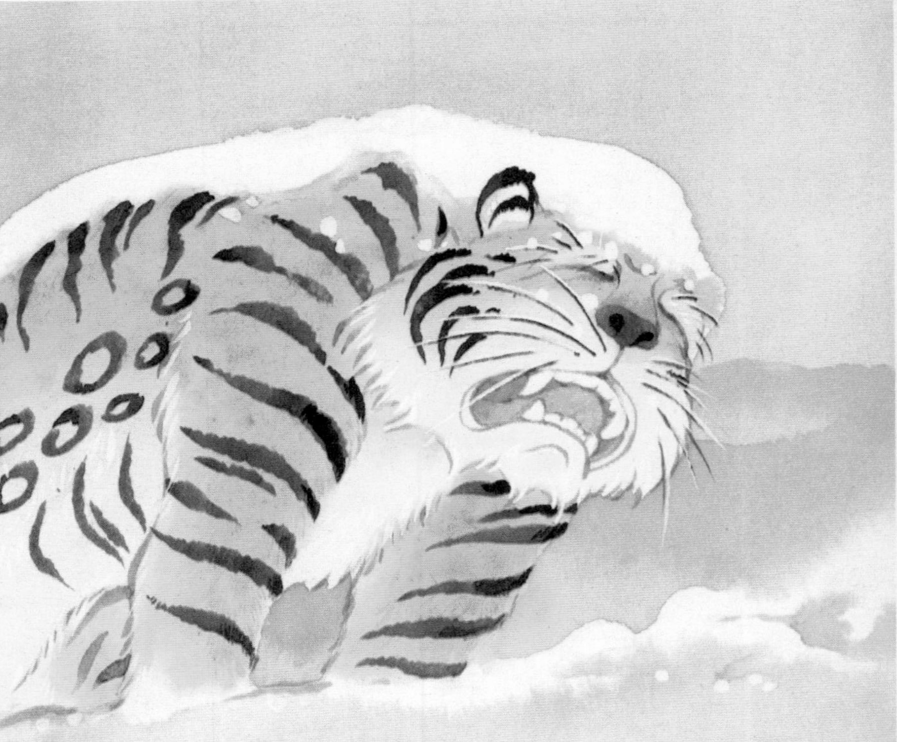

Tiger pulled and pulled,
but his tail did not come out.
It was frozen in solid ice!
"I'm going to get you, Rabbit!"
roared Tiger.
But he could not budge at all.

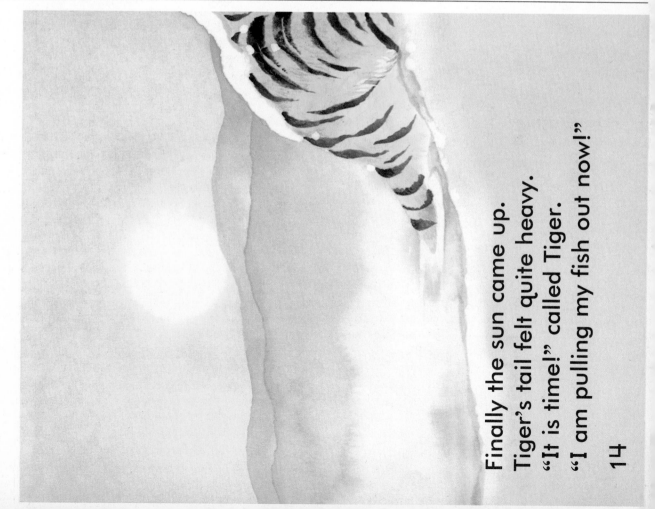

Finally the sun came up.
Tiger's tail felt quite heavy.
"It is time!" called Tiger.
"I am pulling my fish out now!"

The Rabbit and the Tiger

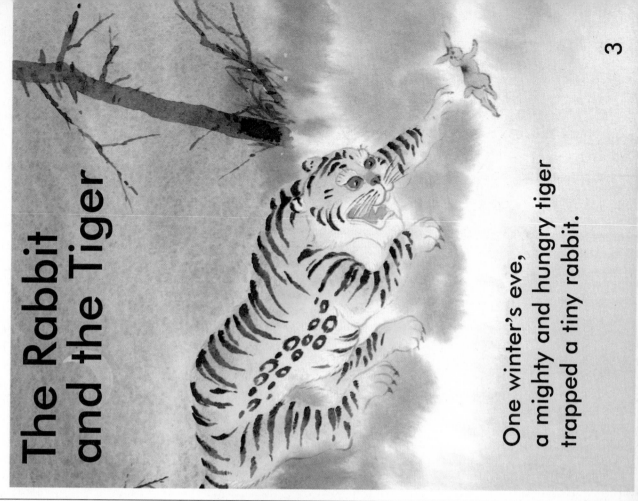

One winter's eve,
a mighty and hungry tiger
trapped a tiny rabbit.

"Do not eat me!" cried Rabbit.
"I am too small to make a good meal.
If you let me go, I will show you
how to catch all the fish you can eat."

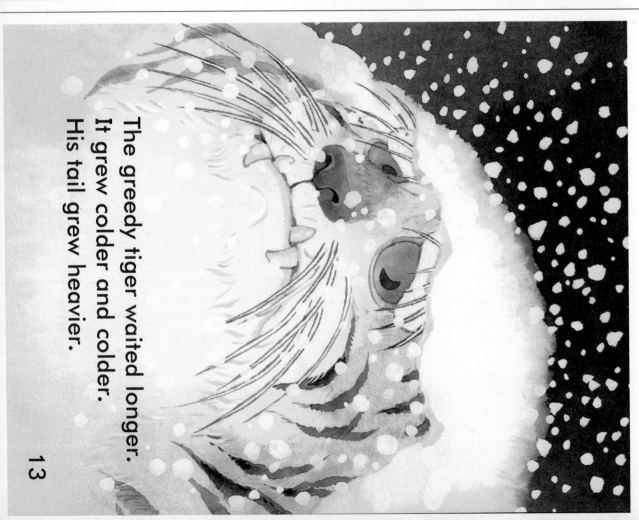

The greedy tiger waited longer.
It grew colder and colder.
His tail grew heavier.

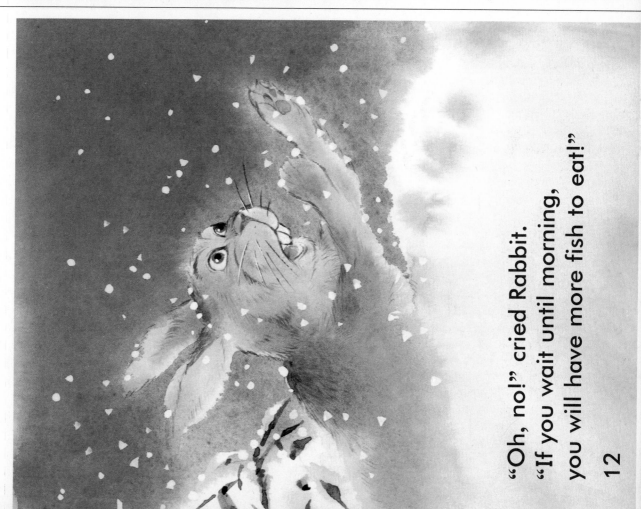

"Oh, no!" cried Rabbit.
"If you wait until morning,
you will have more fish to eat!"

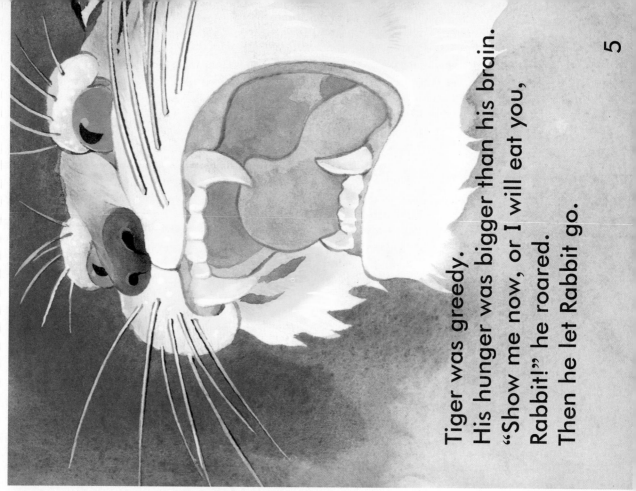

Tiger was greedy.
His hunger was bigger than his brain.
"Show me now, or I will eat you,
Rabbit!" he roared.
Then he let Rabbit go.

Rabbit led Tiger down to a river.
Rabbit told Tiger, "Put your tail in the water."

The Rabbit's Trick

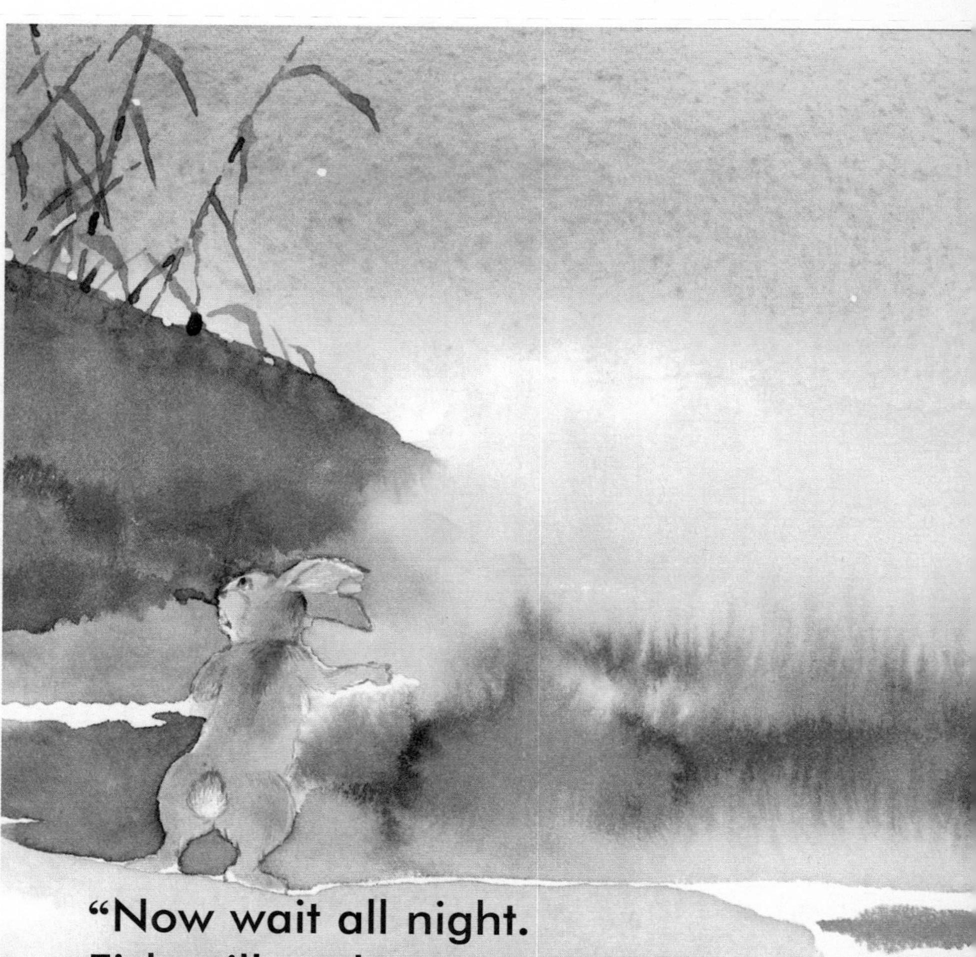

"Is your tail getting heavy?"
called Rabbit.

"Oh yes!" replied Tiger.
"I must be catching lots of fish!
Should I pull my tail out now?"

"Now wait all night.
Fish will grab onto your tail.
Soon your tail will grow heavy.
Then you can pull it out
and eat all the fish!"

"I'll stay close by," whispered Rabbit.
"I will let you know when
you have caught plenty of fish."
Rabbit climbed up the riverbank,
sat down and watched Tiger.

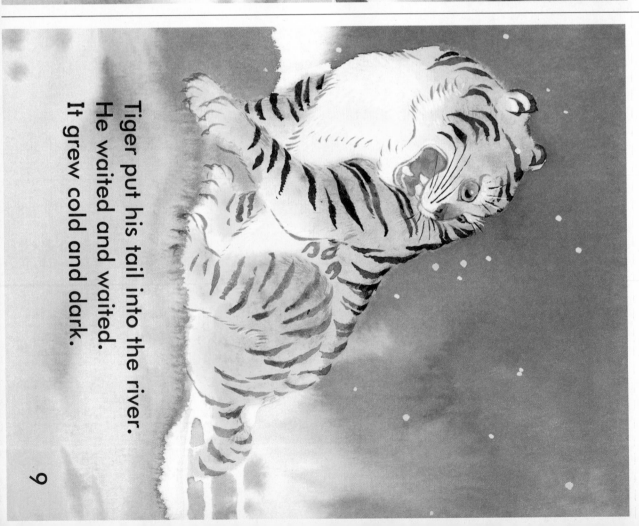

Tiger put his tail into the river.
He waited and waited.
It grew cold and dark.